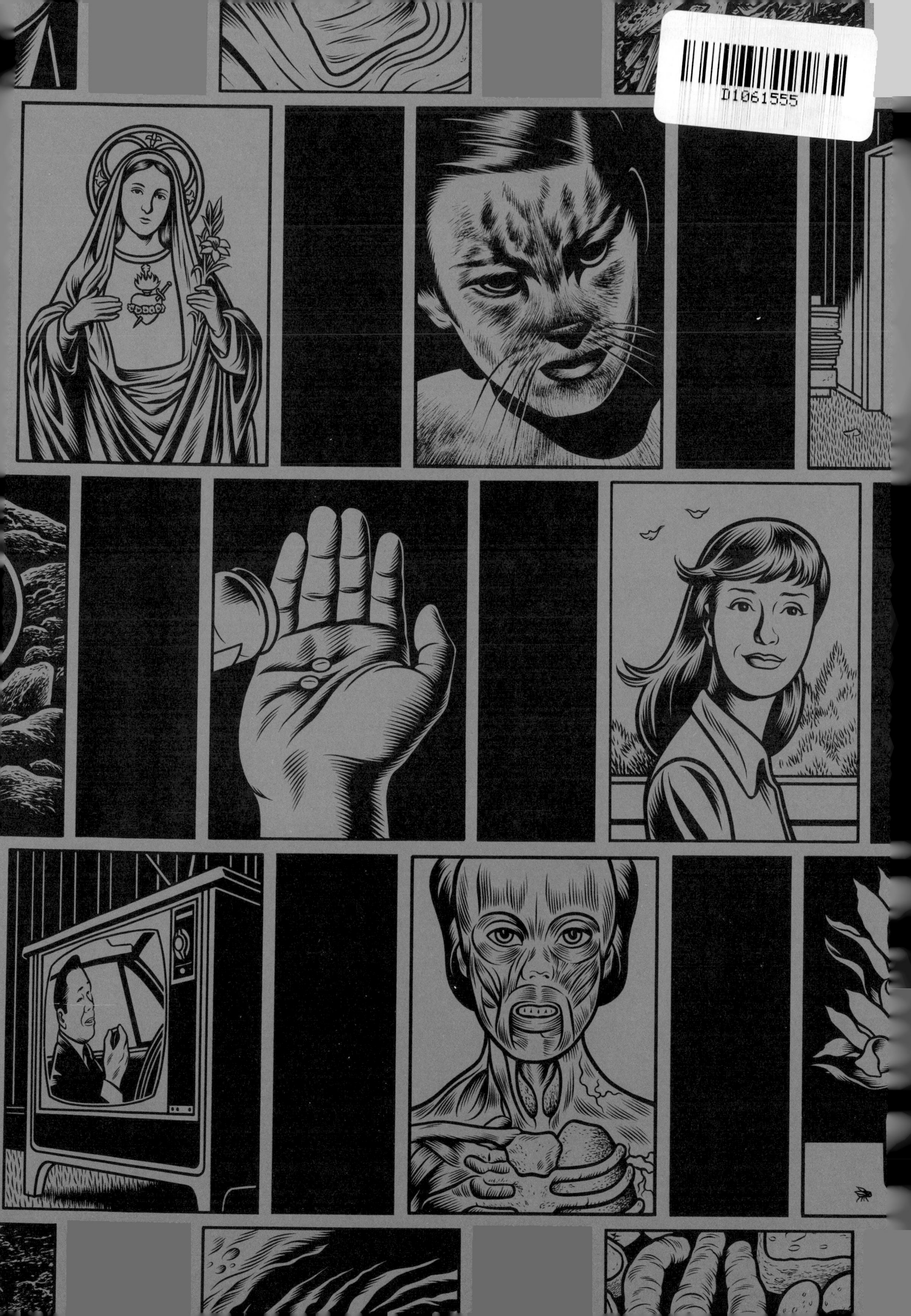

**DATE DUE**

| | | | |
|---|---|---|---|
| | | | |
| | | | |
| | | | |
| | | | |
| | | | |
| | | | |
| | | | |
| | | | |
| | | | |
| | | | |
| | | | |

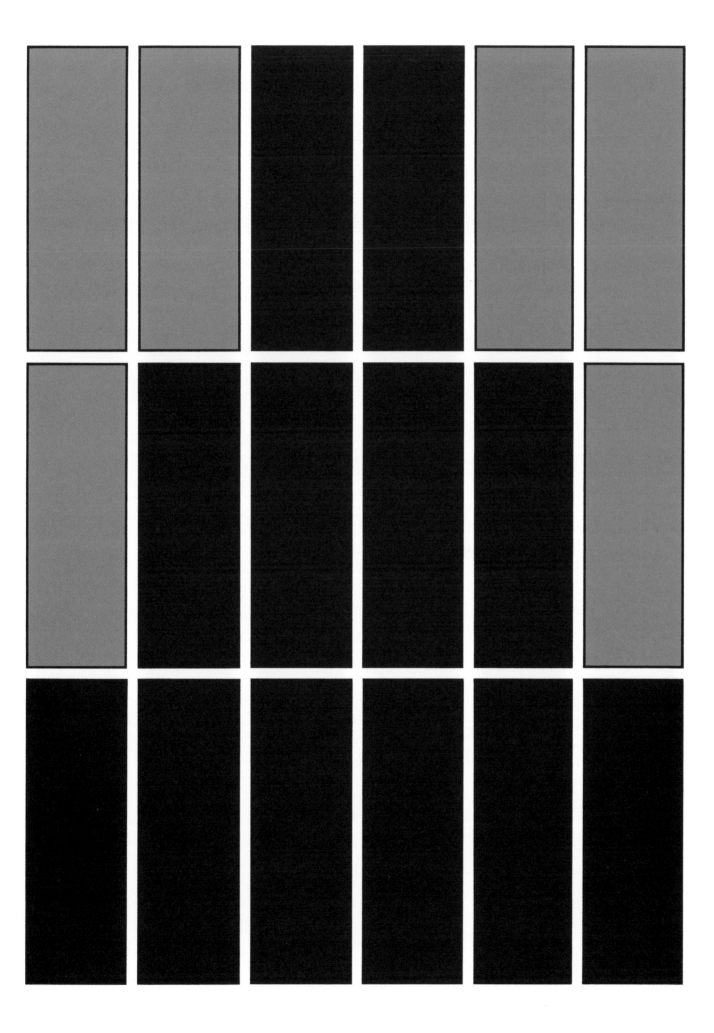

THIS IS A WORK OF FICTION. NAMES, CHARACTERS, PLACES, AND INCIDENTS, EITHER ARE THE PRODUCT OF THE AUTHOR'S IMAGINATION OR ARE USED FICTITIOUSLY. ANY RESEMBLANCE TO ACTUAL PERSONS, LIVING OR DEAD, EVENTS, OR LOCALES, IS ENTIRELY COINCIDENTAL.

 PUBLISHED IN THE UNITED STATES BY PANTHEON BOOKS, A DIVISION OF RANDOM HOUSE, INC., NEW YORK, AND IN CANADA BY RANDOM HOUSE OF CANADA LIMITED, TORONTO.

PANTHEON BOOKS AND COLOPHON ARE REGISTERED TRADEMARKS OF RANDOM HOUSE, INC.

LIBRARY OF CONGRESS CATALOGING-IN-PUBLICATION DATA

BURNS, CHARLES.
THE HIVE / CHARLES BURNS.
P. CM.
ISBN 978-0-307-90788-2
1. GRAPHIC NOVELS. I. TITLE.
PN6727.B87H58 2012
741.5'973—DC23 2012002185

WWW.PANTHEONBOOKS.COM

PRINTED IN CHINA

FIRST EDITION

9 8 7 6 5 4 3 2 1

# CHARLES BURNS
# THE HIVE

# PANTHEON BOOKS
### NEW YORK

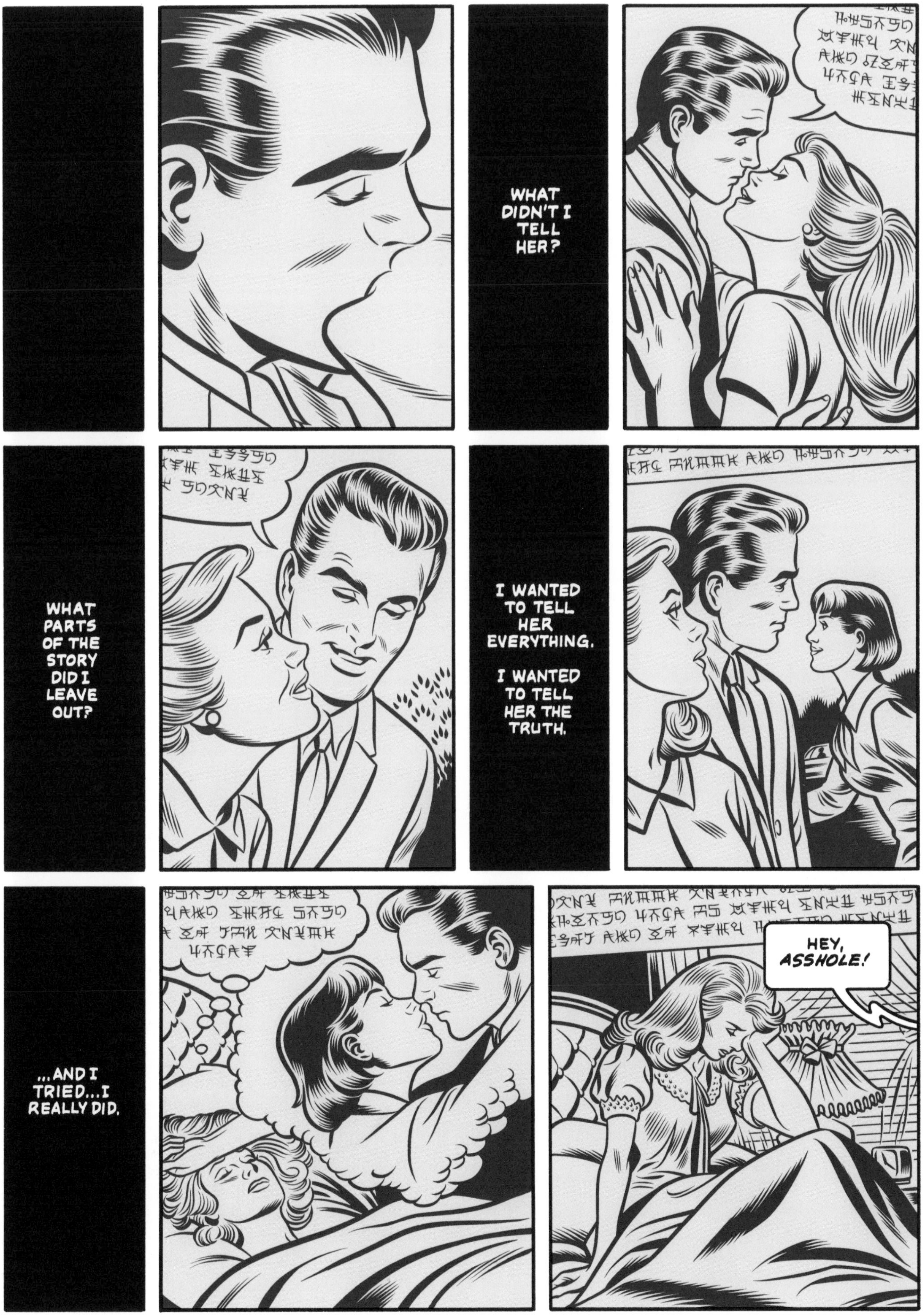
WHAT DIDN'T I TELL HER?
WHAT PARTS OF THE STORY DID I LEAVE OUT?
I WANTED TO TELL HER EVERYTHING.
I WANTED TO TELL HER THE TRUTH.
...AND I TRIED...I REALLY DID.
HEY, ASSHOLE!

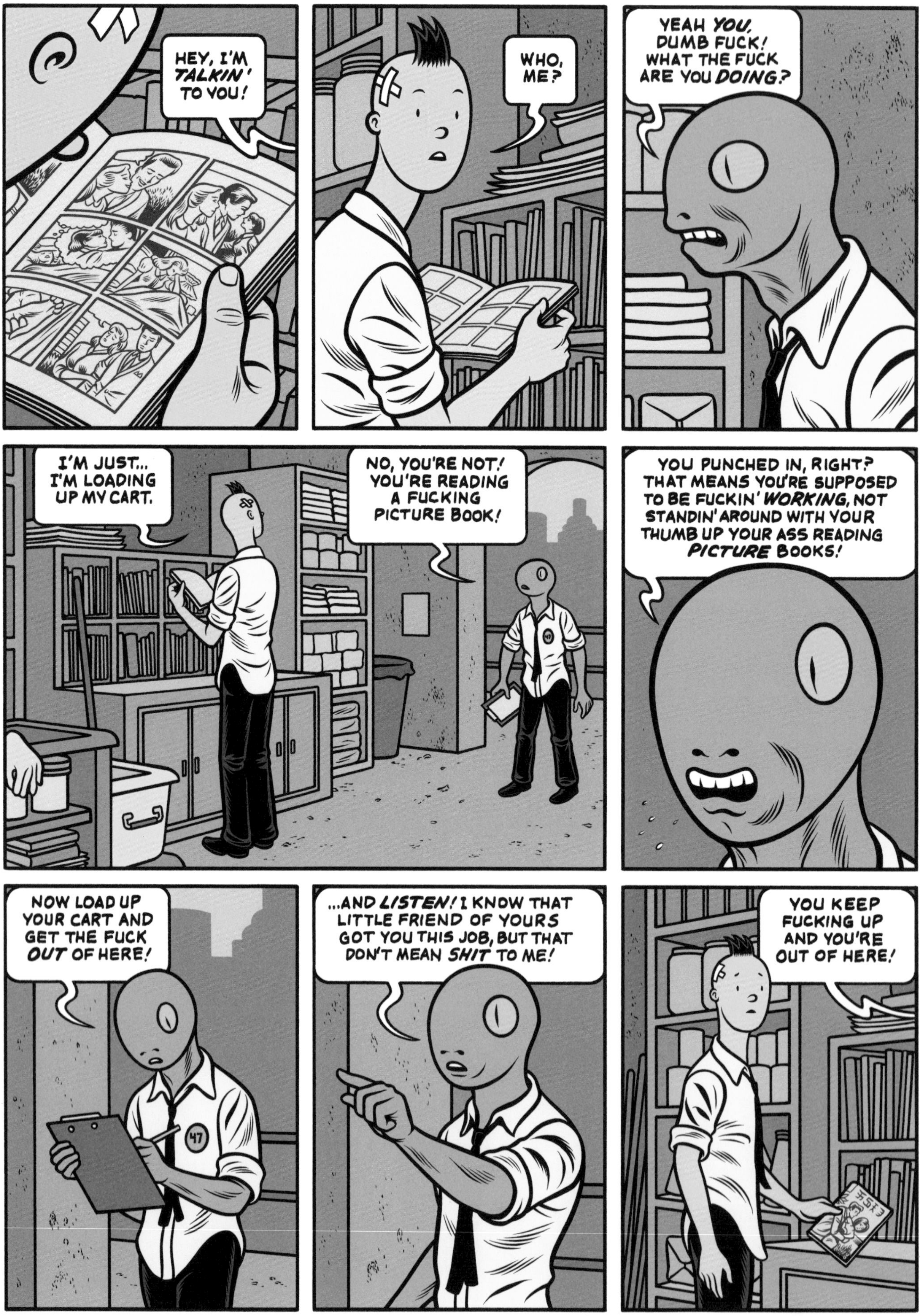
HEY, I'M TALKIN' TO YOU!
WHO, ME?
YEAH YOU, DUMB FUCK! WHAT THE FUCK ARE YOU DOING?
I'M JUST... I'M LOADING UP MY CART.
NO, YOU'RE NOT! YOU'RE READING A FUCKING PICTURE BOOK!
YOU PUNCHED IN, RIGHT? THAT MEANS YOU'RE SUPPOSED TO BE FUCKIN' WORKING, NOT STANDIN' AROUND WITH YOUR THUMB UP YOUR ASS READING PICTURE BOOKS!
NOW LOAD UP YOUR CART AND GET THE FUCK OUT OF HERE!
...AND LISTEN! I KNOW THAT LITTLE FRIEND OF YOURS GOT YOU THIS JOB, BUT THAT DON'T MEAN SHIT TO ME!
YOU KEEP FUCKING UP AND YOU'RE OUT OF HERE!

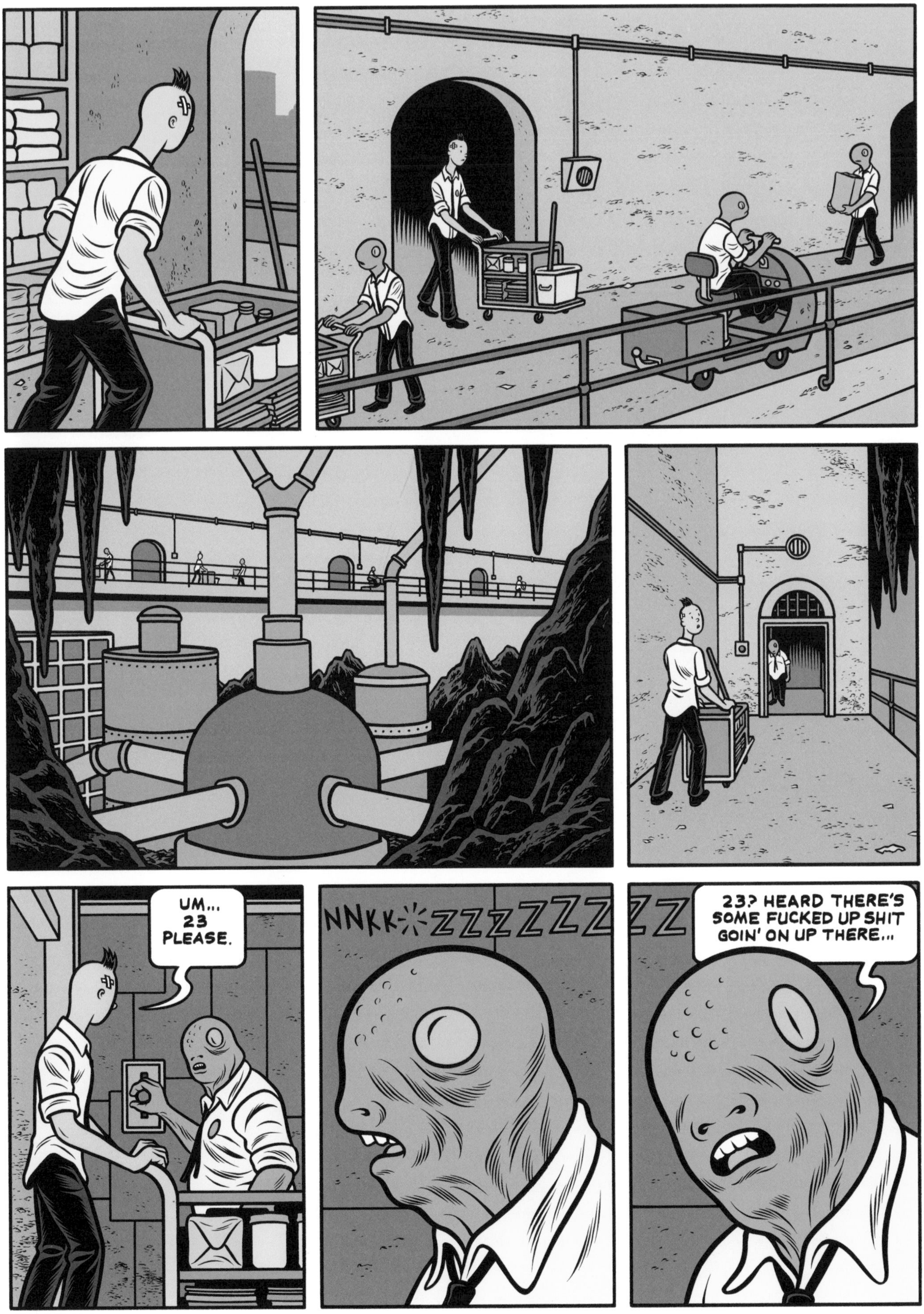
UM... 23 PLEASE.
NNKK-ZZZZZZZZZZ
23? HEARD THERE'S SOME FUCKED UP SHIT GOIN' ON UP THERE...

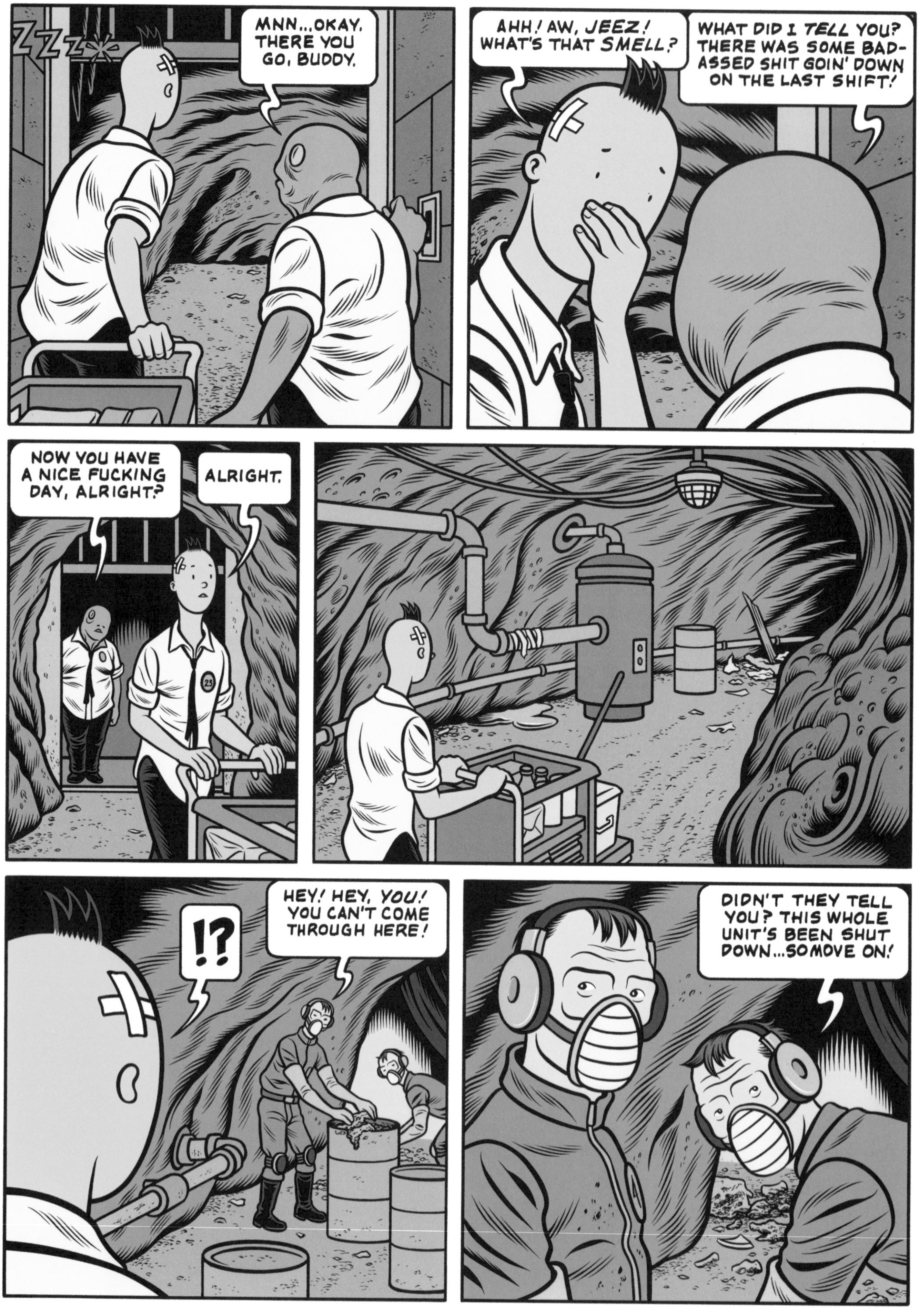
ZZZ
MNN...OKAY. THERE YOU GO, BUDDY.
AHH! AW, JEEZ! WHAT'S THAT SMELL?
WHAT DID I TELL YOU? THERE WAS SOME BAD-ASSED SHIT GOIN' DOWN ON THE LAST SHIFT!
NOW YOU HAVE A NICE FUCKING DAY, ALRIGHT?
ALRIGHT.
!?
HEY! HEY, YOU! YOU CAN'T COME THROUGH HERE!
DIDN'T THEY TELL YOU? THIS WHOLE UNIT'S BEEN SHUT DOWN...SO MOVE ON!

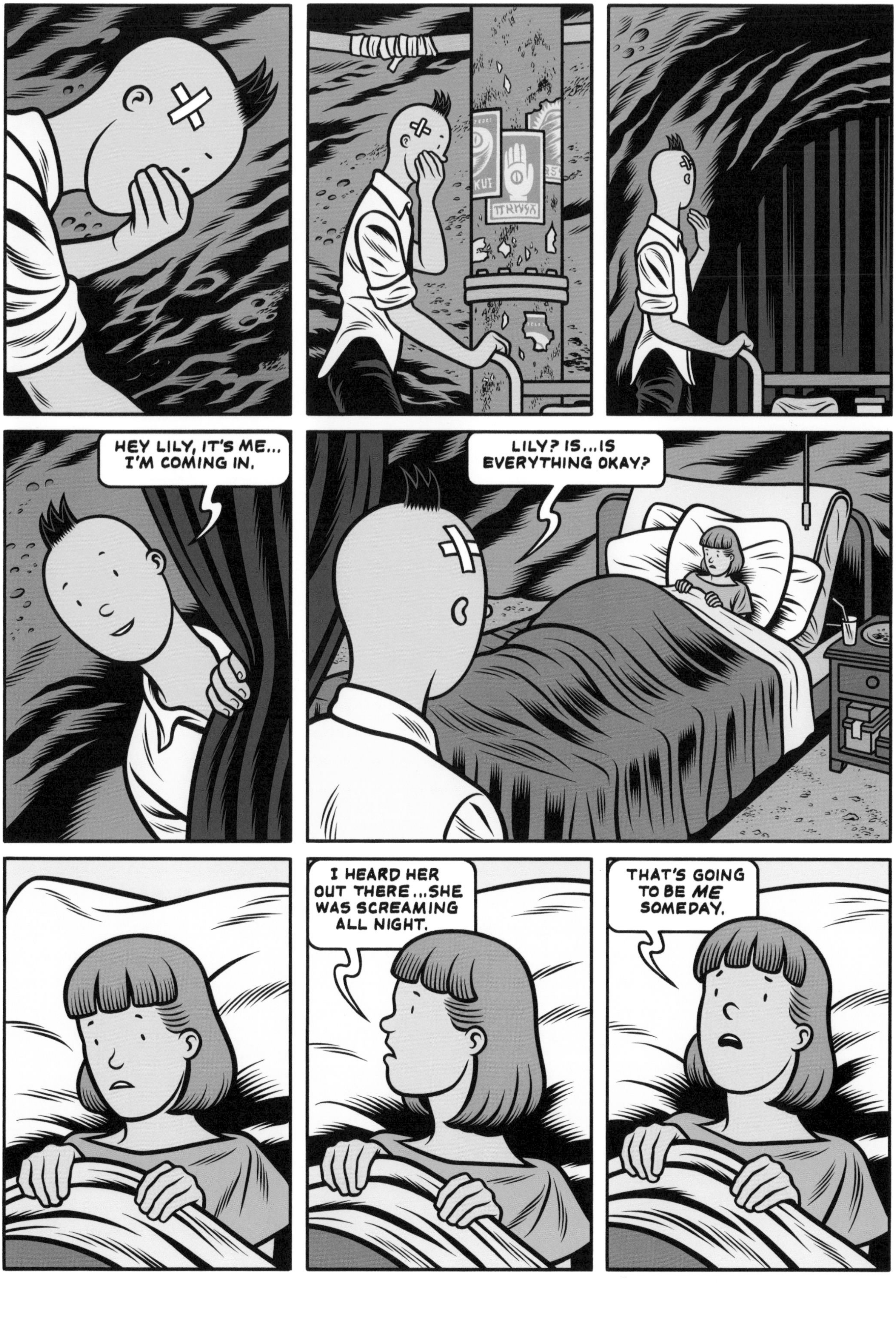
HEY LILY, IT'S ME... I'M COMING IN.
LILY? IS...IS EVERYTHING OKAY?
I HEARD HER OUT THERE...SHE WAS SCREAMING ALL NIGHT.
THAT'S GOING TO BE *ME* SOMEDAY.

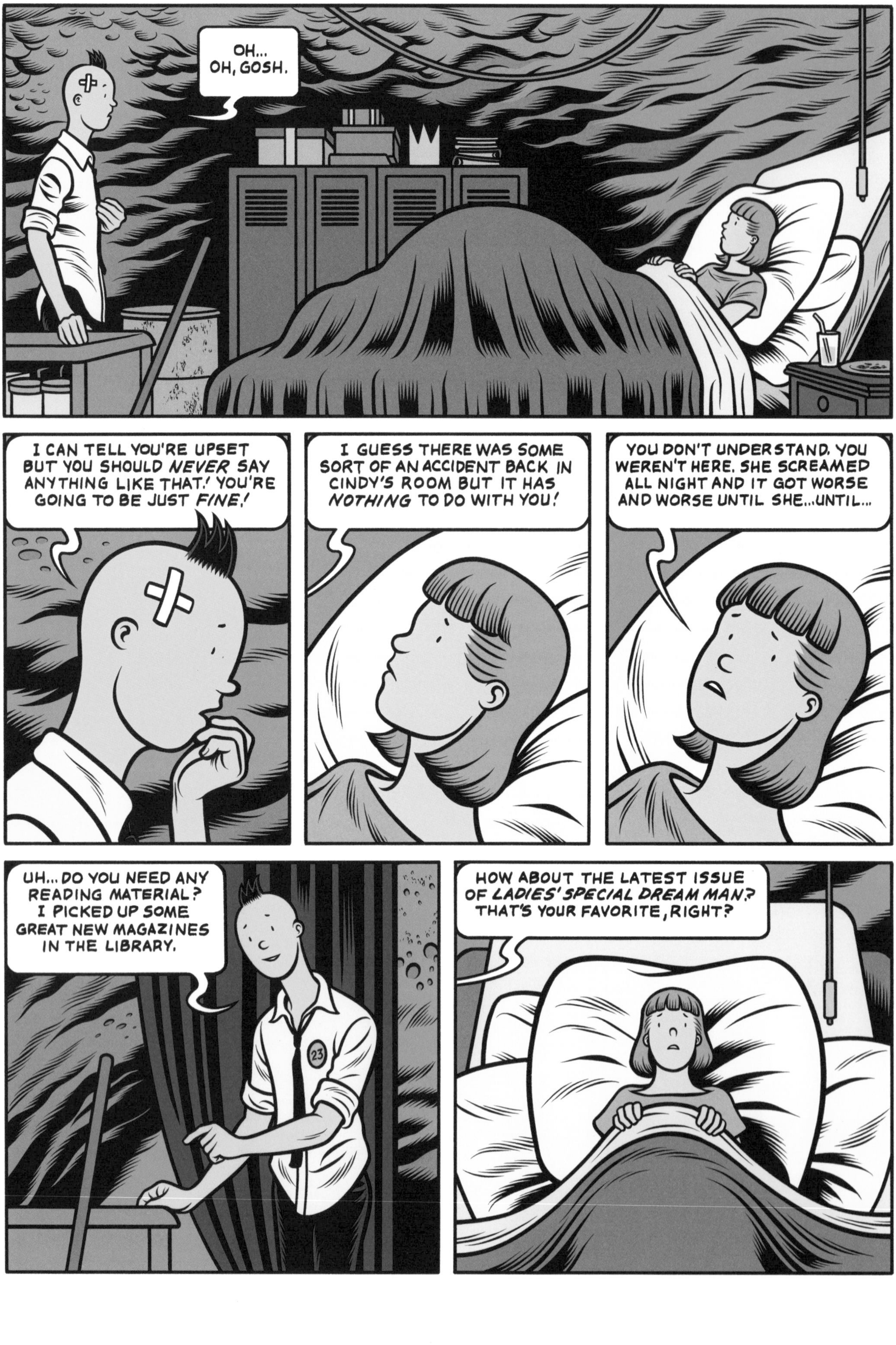
OH... OH, GOSH.
I CAN TELL YOU'RE UPSET BUT YOU SHOULD *NEVER* SAY ANYTHING LIKE THAT! YOU'RE GOING TO BE JUST *FINE!*
I GUESS THERE WAS SOME SORT OF AN ACCIDENT BACK IN CINDY'S ROOM BUT IT HAS *NOTHING* TO DO WITH YOU!
YOU DON'T UNDERSTAND. YOU WEREN'T HERE. SHE SCREAMED ALL NIGHT AND IT GOT WORSE AND WORSE UNTIL SHE...UNTIL...
UH... DO YOU NEED ANY READING MATERIAL? I PICKED UP SOME GREAT NEW MAGAZINES IN THE LIBRARY.
23
HOW ABOUT THE LATEST ISSUE OF *LADIES' SPECIAL DREAM MAN?* THAT'S YOUR FAVORITE, RIGHT?

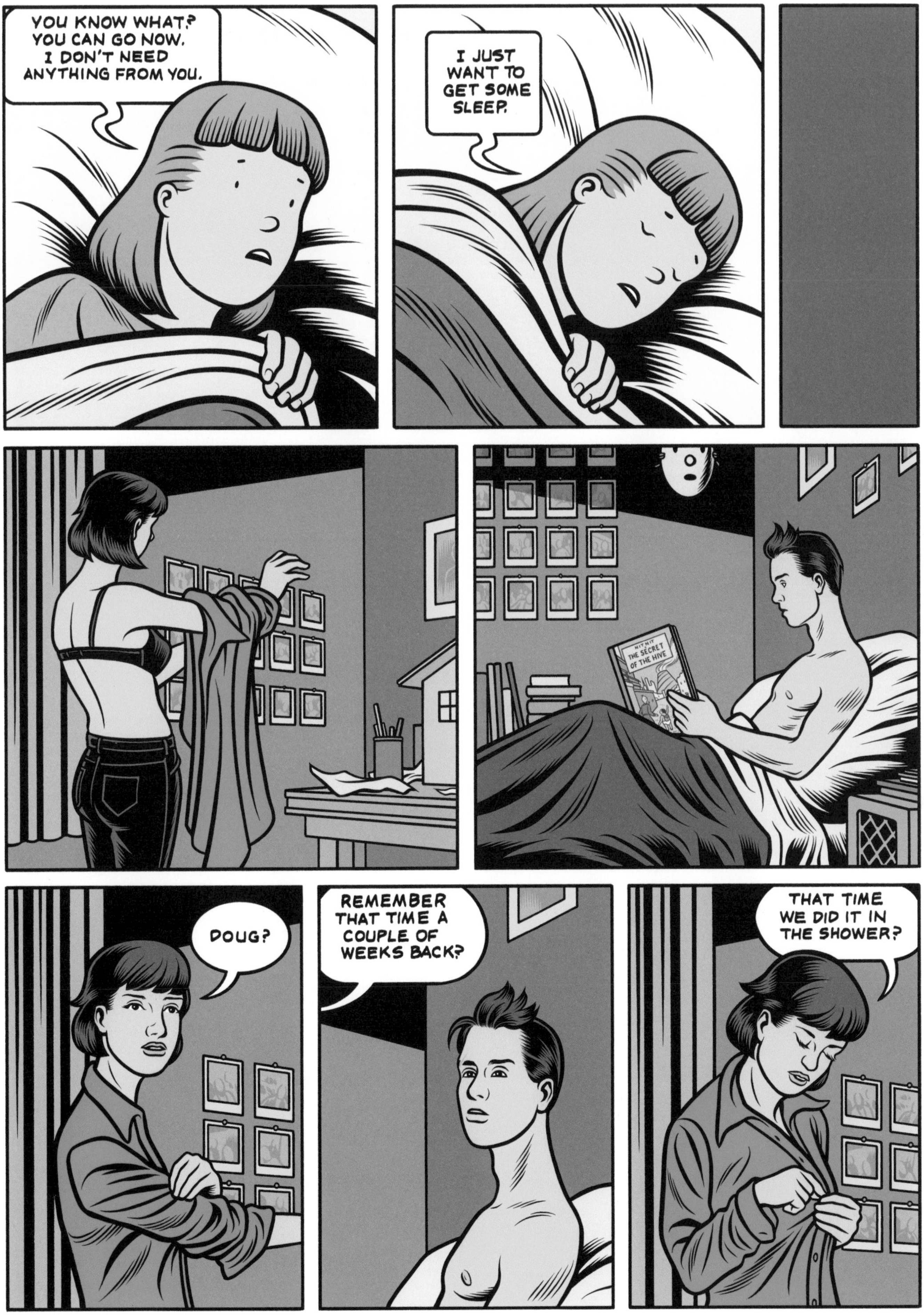

YOU KNOW WHAT? YOU CAN GO NOW. I DON'T NEED ANYTHING FROM YOU.
I JUST WANT TO GET SOME SLEEP.
THE SECRET OF THE HIVE
DOUG?
REMEMBER THAT TIME A COUPLE OF WEEKS BACK?
THAT TIME WE DID IT IN THE SHOWER?

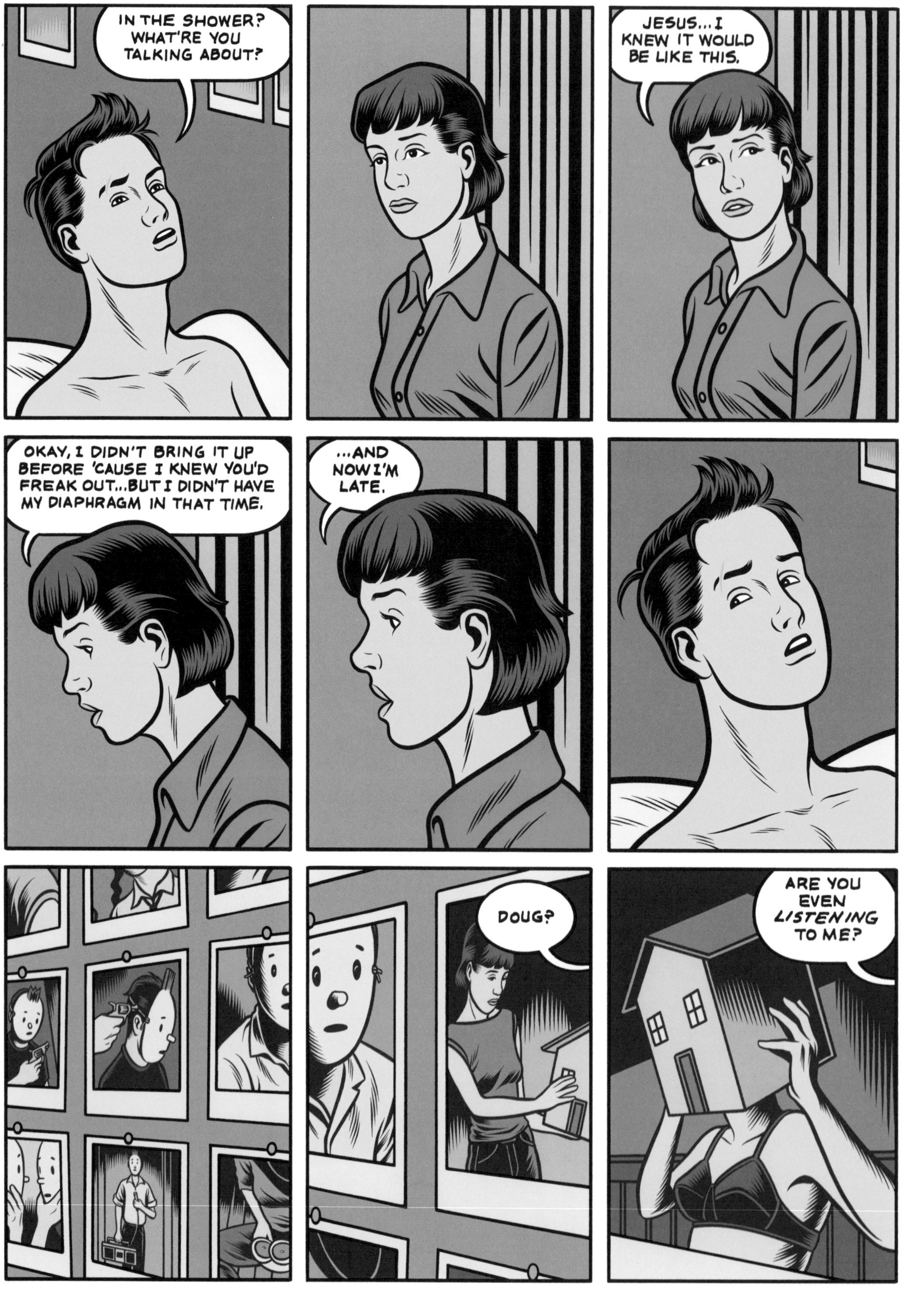
IN THE SHOWER? WHAT'RE YOU TALKING ABOUT?
JESUS...I KNEW IT WOULD BE LIKE THIS.
OKAY, I DIDN'T BRING IT UP BEFORE 'CAUSE I KNEW YOU'D FREAK OUT...BUT I DIDN'T HAVE MY DIAPHRAGM IN THAT TIME.
...AND NOW I'M LATE.
DOUG?
ARE YOU EVEN *LISTENING* TO ME?

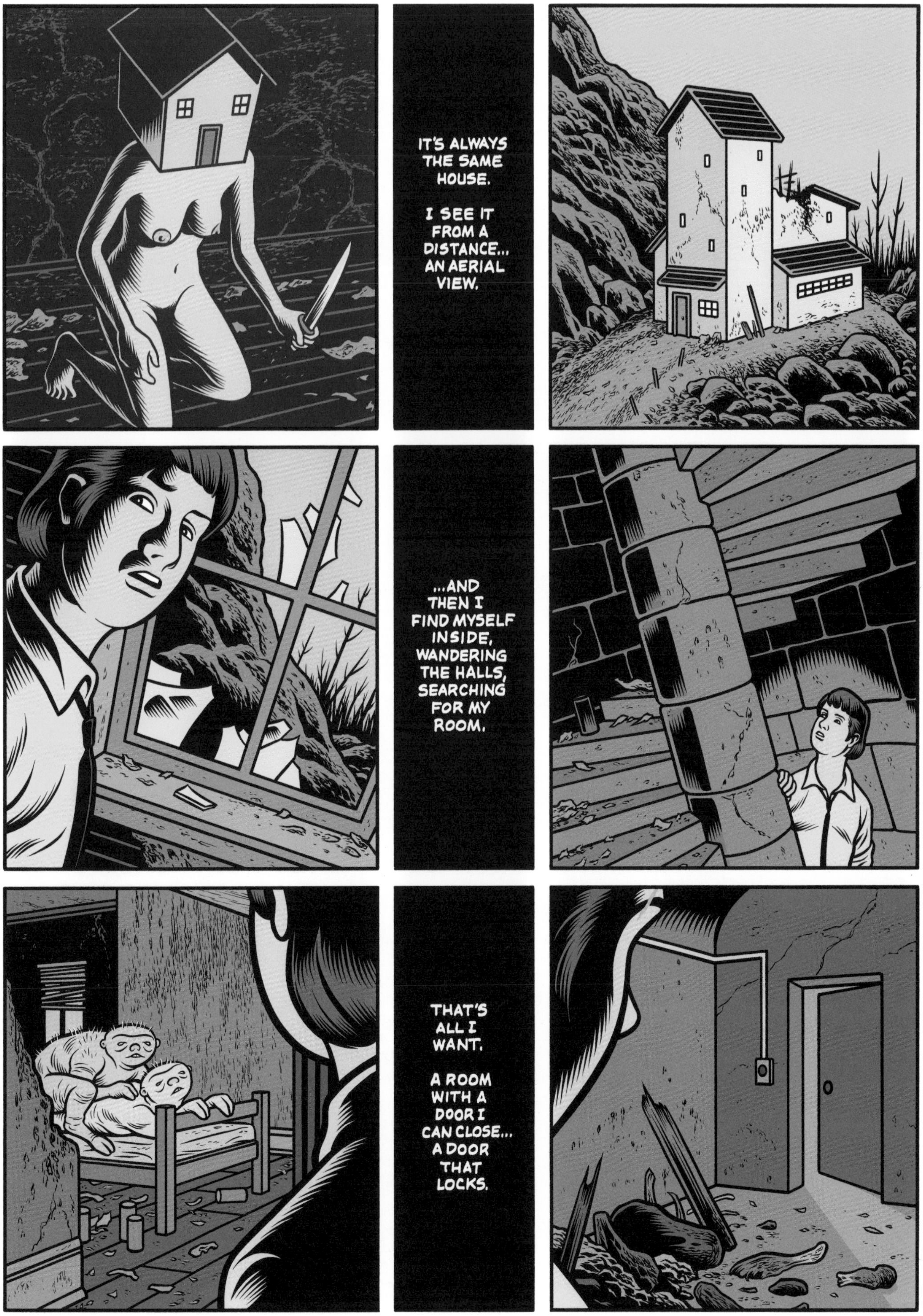
IT'S ALWAYS THE SAME HOUSE.
I SEE IT FROM A DISTANCE... AN AERIAL VIEW.
...AND THEN I FIND MYSELF INSIDE, WANDERING THE HALLS, SEARCHING FOR MY ROOM.
THAT'S ALL I WANT.
A ROOM WITH A DOOR I CAN CLOSE... A DOOR THAT LOCKS.

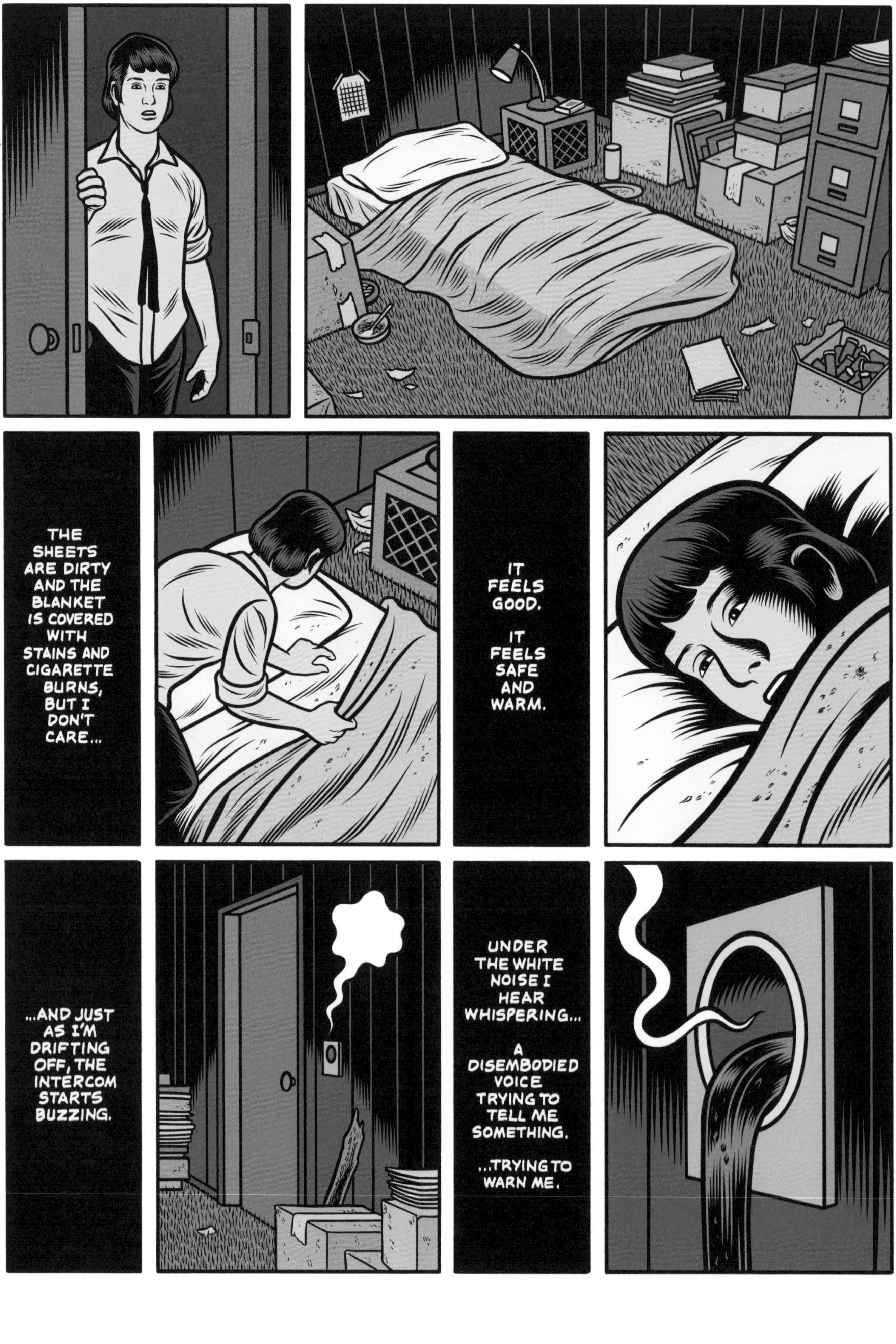
THE SHEETS ARE DIRTY AND THE BLANKET IS COVERED WITH STAINS AND CIGARETTE BURNS, BUT I DON'T CARE...
IT FEELS GOOD.
IT FEELS SAFE AND WARM.
...AND JUST AS I'M DRIFTING OFF, THE INTERCOM STARTS BUZZING.
UNDER THE WHITE NOISE I HEAR WHISPERING...
A DISEMBODIED VOICE TRYING TO TELL ME SOMETHING.
...TRYING TO WARN ME.

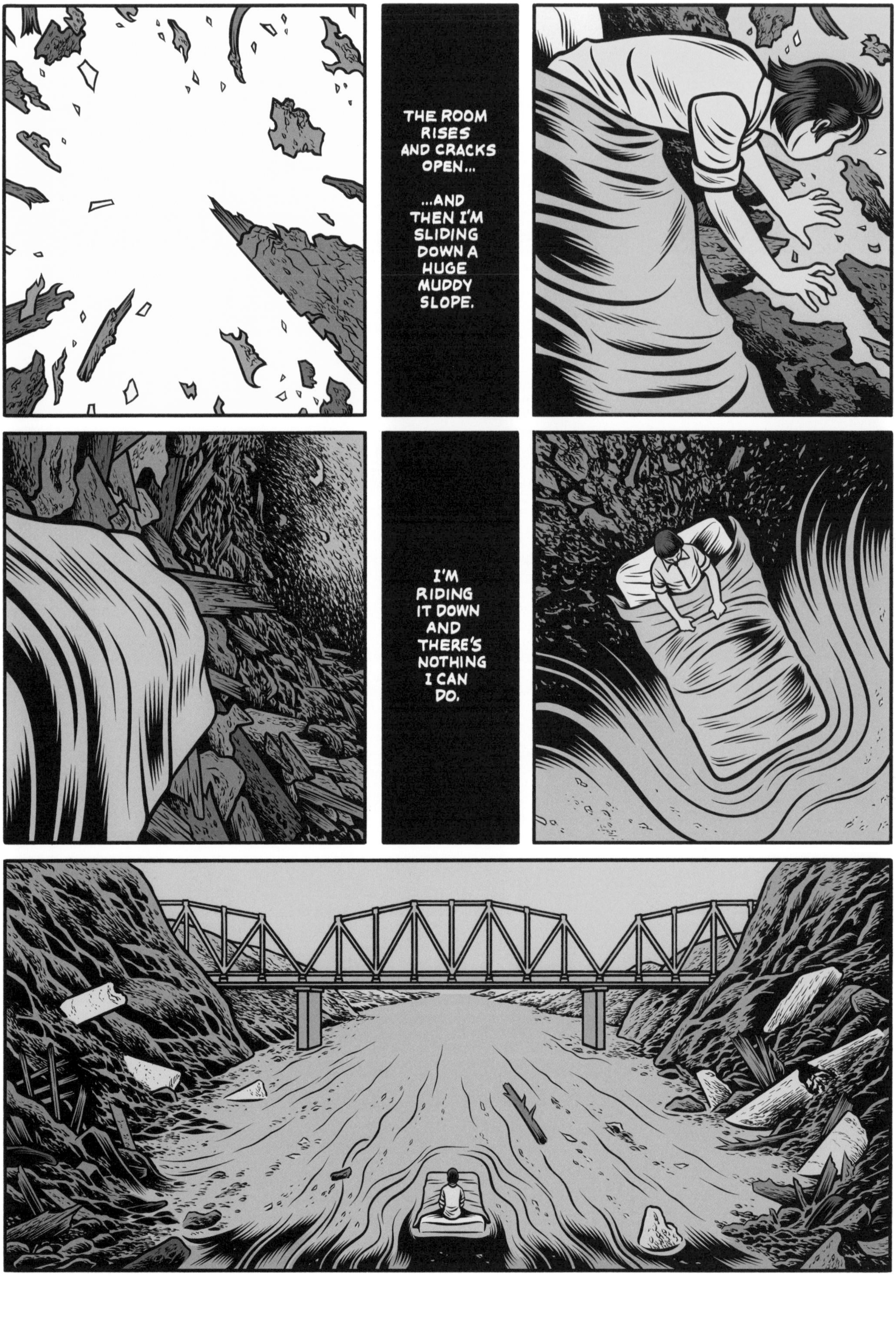
THE ROOM RISES AND CRACKS OPEN...
...AND THEN I'M SLIDING DOWN A HUGE MUDDY SLOPE.
I'M RIDING IT DOWN AND THERE'S NOTHING I CAN DO.

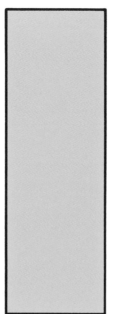

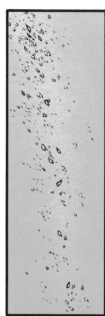

OH, OKAY...NOW I REMEMBER... I WAS GOING TO TELL YOU ABOUT TAKING MY DAD'S ASHES AND THROWING THEM OFF A BRIDGE.

DID I EVER TELL YOU ABOUT THAT?

YEAH, YOU DID. ACTUALLY, YOU'VE TOLD ME A COUPLE OF TIMES.

I DID? AW, WELL FUCK ME...

I TRY TO CONTROL IT...

TRY TO FOCUS IN ON THE GOOD THINGS.

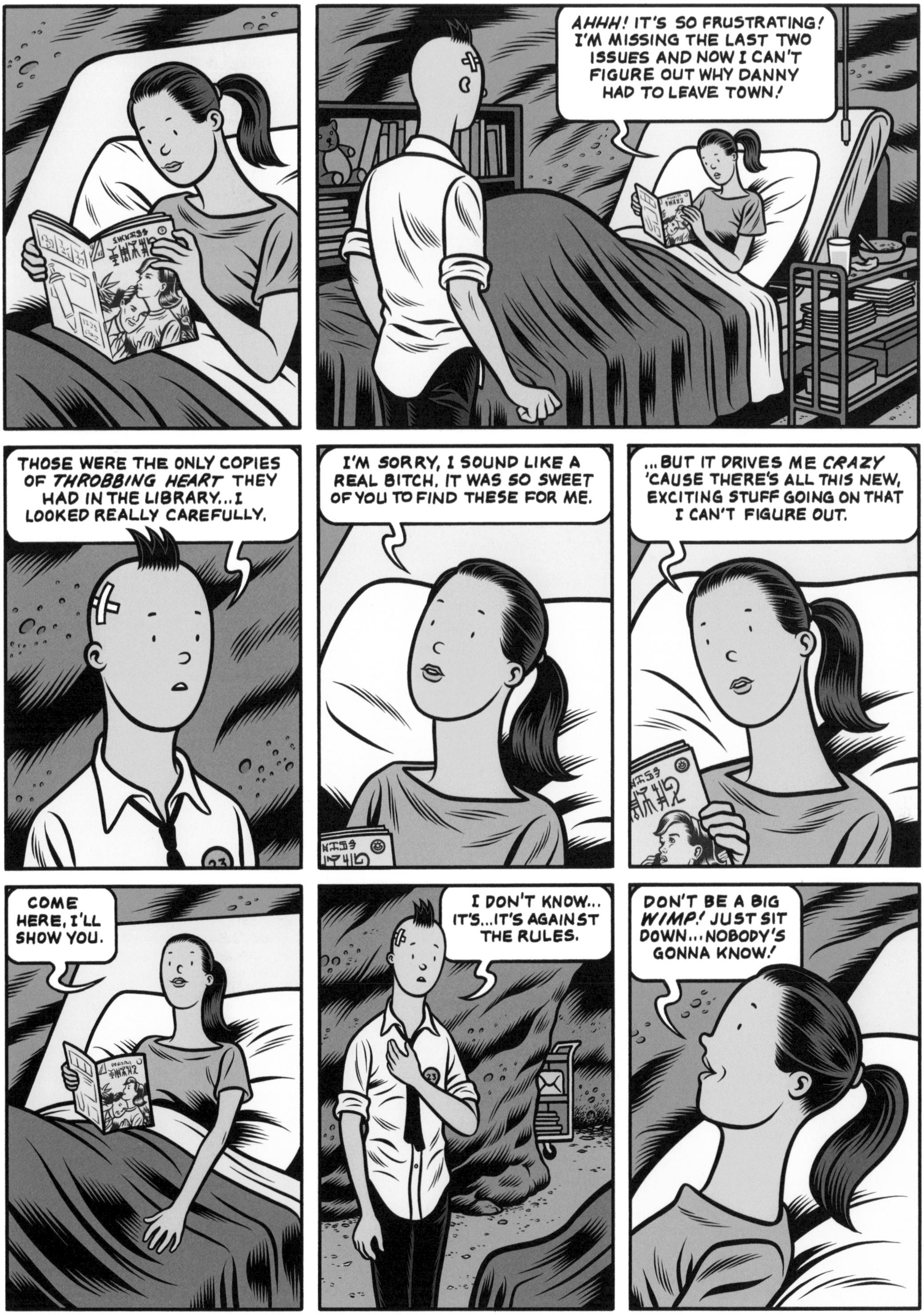
AHHH! IT'S SO FRUSTRATING! I'M MISSING THE LAST TWO ISSUES AND NOW I CAN'T FIGURE OUT WHY DANNY HAD TO LEAVE TOWN!
THOSE WERE THE ONLY COPIES OF THROBBING HEART THEY HAD IN THE LIBRARY...I LOOKED REALLY CAREFULLY.
I'M SORRY, I SOUND LIKE A REAL BITCH. IT WAS SO SWEET OF YOU TO FIND THESE FOR ME.
...BUT IT DRIVES ME CRAZY 'CAUSE THERE'S ALL THIS NEW, EXCITING STUFF GOING ON THAT I CAN'T FIGURE OUT.
COME HERE, I'LL SHOW YOU.
I DON'T KNOW... IT'S...IT'S AGAINST THE RULES.
DON'T BE A BIG WIMP! JUST SIT DOWN...NOBODY'S GONNA KNOW!

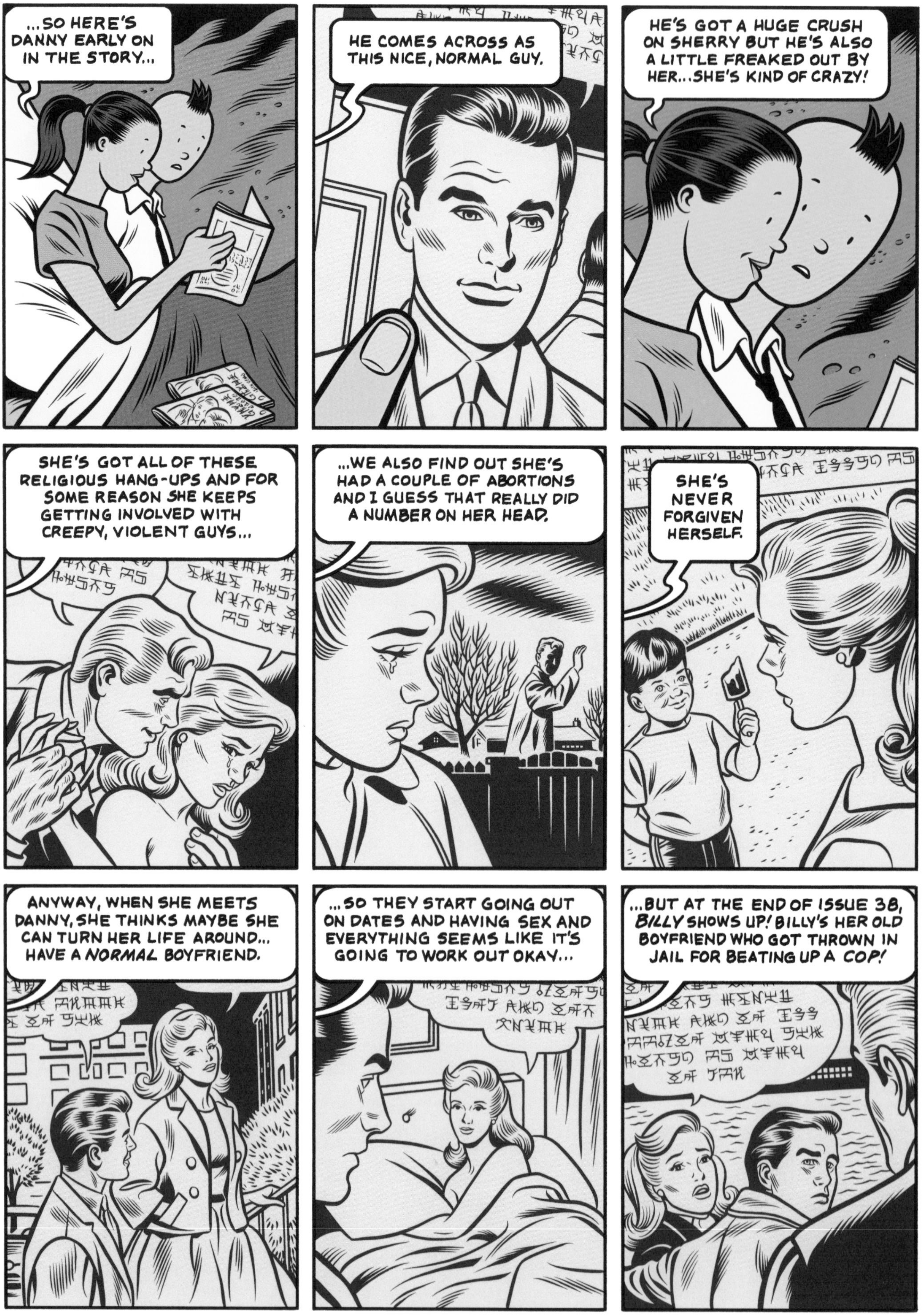
...SO HERE'S DANNY EARLY ON IN THE STORY...
HE COMES ACROSS AS THIS NICE, NORMAL GUY.
HE'S GOT A HUGE CRUSH ON SHERRY BUT HE'S ALSO A LITTLE FREAKED OUT BY HER...SHE'S KIND OF CRAZY!
SHE'S GOT ALL OF THESE RELIGIOUS HANG-UPS AND FOR SOME REASON SHE KEEPS GETTING INVOLVED WITH CREEPY, VIOLENT GUYS...
...WE ALSO FIND OUT SHE'S HAD A COUPLE OF ABORTIONS AND I GUESS THAT REALLY DID A NUMBER ON HER HEAD.
SHE'S NEVER FORGIVEN HERSELF.
ANYWAY, WHEN SHE MEETS DANNY, SHE THINKS MAYBE SHE CAN TURN HER LIFE AROUND... HAVE A *NORMAL* BOYFRIEND.
...SO THEY START GOING OUT ON DATES AND HAVING SEX AND EVERYTHING SEEMS LIKE IT'S GOING TO WORK OUT OKAY...
...BUT AT THE END OF ISSUE 38, *BILLY* SHOWS UP! BILLY'S HER OLD BOYFRIEND WHO GOT THROWN IN JAIL FOR BEATING UP A *COP*!

THEN WE SKIP TO ISSUE 41 AND LOOK! EVERYTHING HAS TOTALLY CHANGED!
DANNY'S ALL MESSED UP... HE'S LEFT TOWN AND MOVED BACK INTO HIS PARENTS' HOUSE.
HIS HEAD'S BANDAGED UP AND HE'S TAKING A WHOLE BUNCH OF HEAVY-DUTY NARCOTICS.
IT'S PRETTY OBVIOUS THAT SOMETHING REALLY, REALLY AWFUL HAPPENED, BUT WHAT? IT'S DRIVING ME NUTS!
I...I'LL TRY TO FIND THOSE ISSUES FOR YOU, OKAY?
I'LL TRY MY BEST.

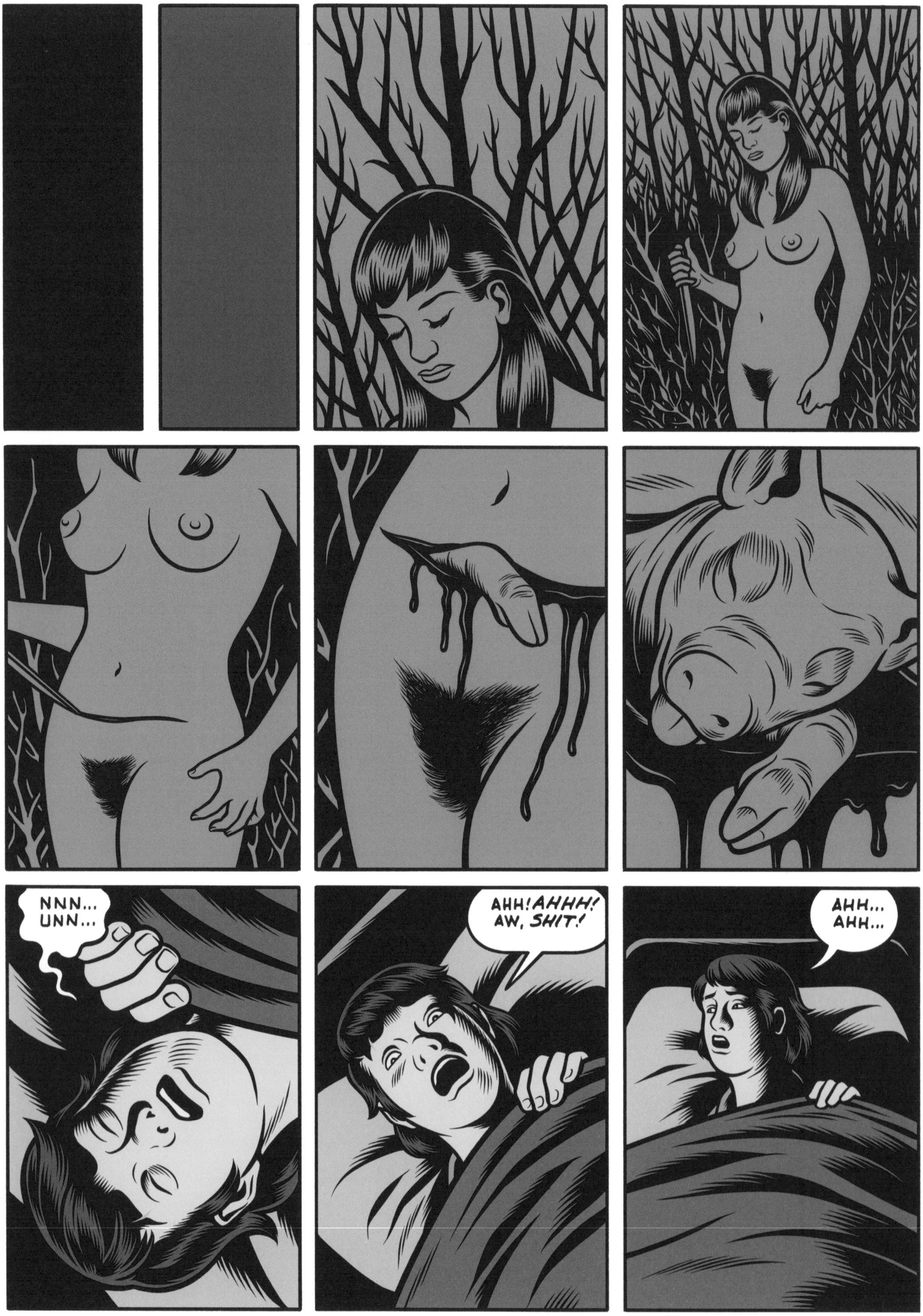
NNN... UNN...
AHH! AHHH! AW, SHIT!
AHH... AHH...

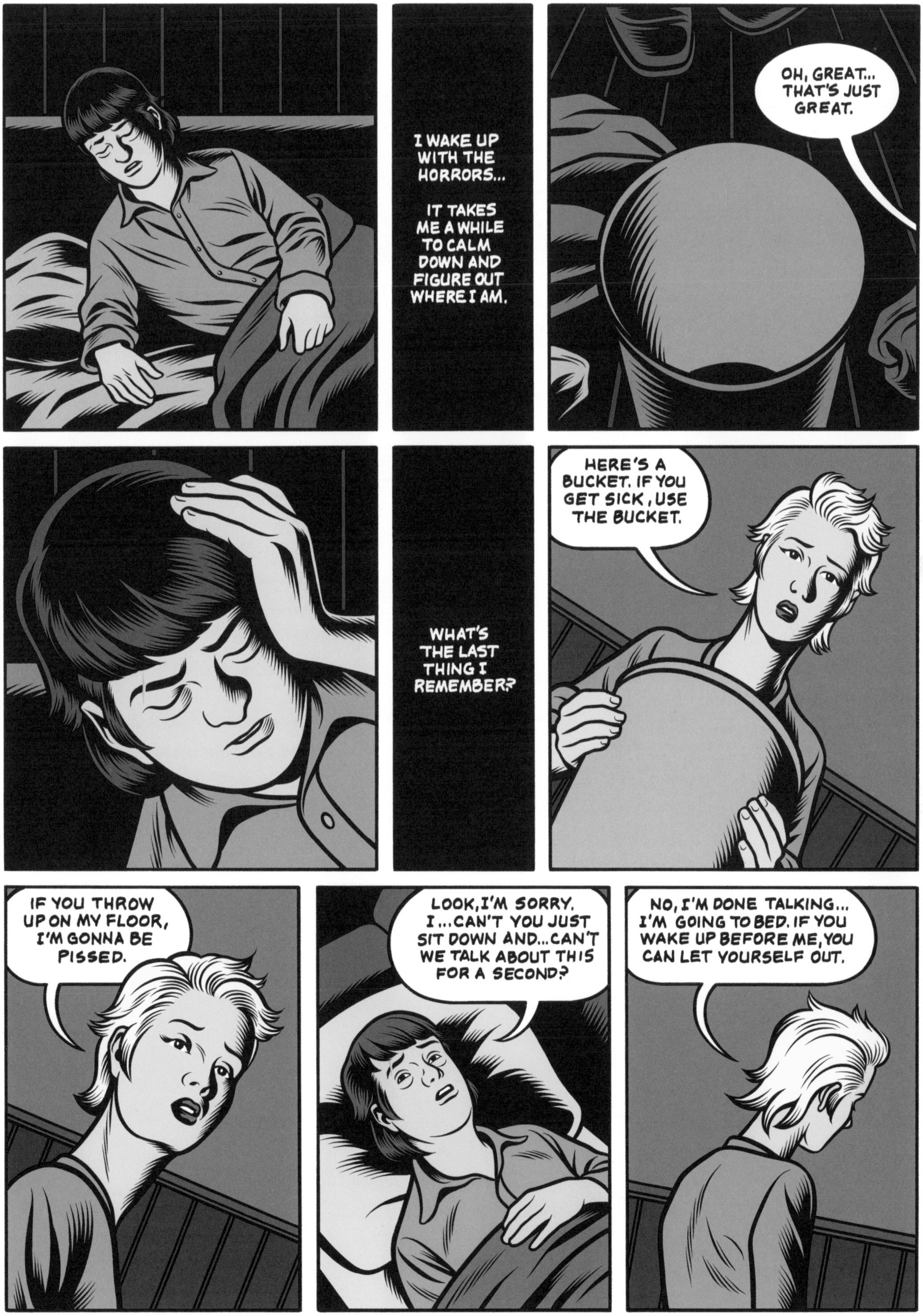
I WAKE UP WITH THE HORRORS...
IT TAKES ME A WHILE TO CALM DOWN AND FIGURE OUT WHERE I AM.
OH, GREAT... THAT'S JUST GREAT.
WHAT'S THE LAST THING I REMEMBER?
HERE'S A BUCKET. IF YOU GET SICK, USE THE BUCKET.
IF YOU THROW UP ON MY FLOOR, I'M GONNA BE PISSED.
LOOK, I'M SORRY. I...CAN'T YOU JUST SIT DOWN AND...CAN'T WE TALK ABOUT THIS FOR A SECOND?
NO, I'M DONE TALKING... I'M GOING TO BED. IF YOU WAKE UP BEFORE ME, YOU CAN LET YOURSELF OUT.

THE EVENING STARTED OUT OKAY. I BROUGHT OVER A SIX-PACK OF PABST AND A PINT OF JIM BEAM. I DID MOST OF THE DRINKING.

I ALSO DID MOST OF THE TALKING. I HAD IT IN MY HEAD THAT I WAS GOING TO TELL HER EVERYTHING... THE WHOLE STORY.

...AND I TRIED, I REALLY DID...BUT IT CAME OUT ALL WRONG.

WHAT PARTS DID I LEAVE OUT? WHAT DIDN'T I TELL HER?

I TOLD HER ABOUT THROWING MY DAD'S ASHES OFF THE BRIDGE...

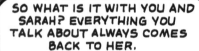

...AND THE COMICS...FINDING THOSE ROMANCE COMICS WITH SARAH.

SO WHAT IS IT WITH YOU AND SARAH? EVERYTHING YOU TALK ABOUT ALWAYS COMES BACK TO HER.

AW, SHIT...YEAH, I GUESS YOU'RE RIGHT. SORRY ABOUT THAT.

THERE'S SOMETHING YOU'RE NOT TELLING ME ABOUT HER... SOMETHING IMPORTANT. I CAN HEAR IT IN YOUR VOICE.

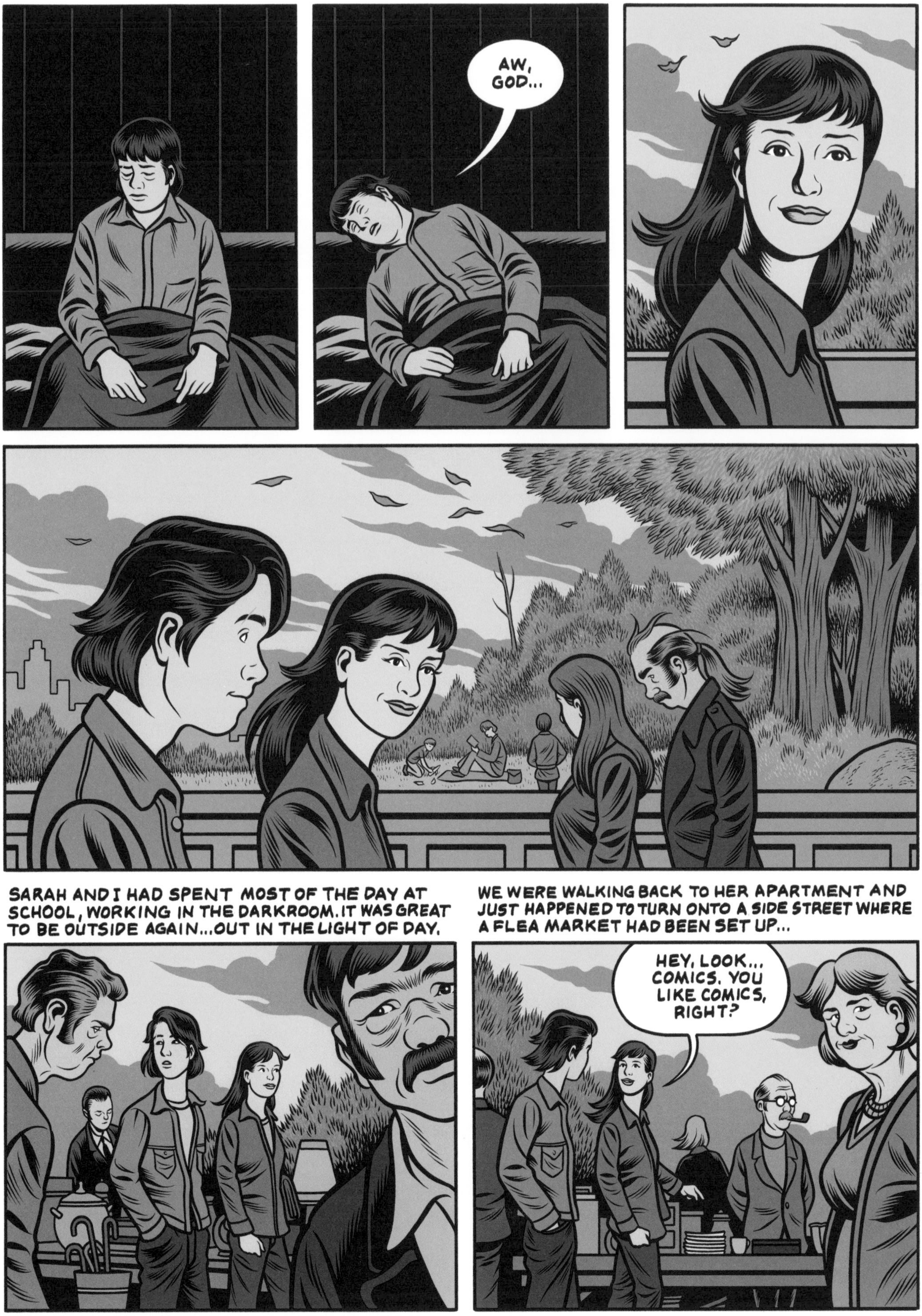
AW, GOD...
SARAH AND I HAD SPENT MOST OF THE DAY AT SCHOOL, WORKING IN THE DARKROOM. IT WAS GREAT TO BE OUTSIDE AGAIN...OUT IN THE LIGHT OF DAY.
WE WERE WALKING BACK TO HER APARTMENT AND JUST HAPPENED TO TURN ONTO A SIDE STREET WHERE A FLEA MARKET HAD BEEN SET UP...
HEY, LOOK... COMICS. YOU LIKE COMICS, RIGHT?

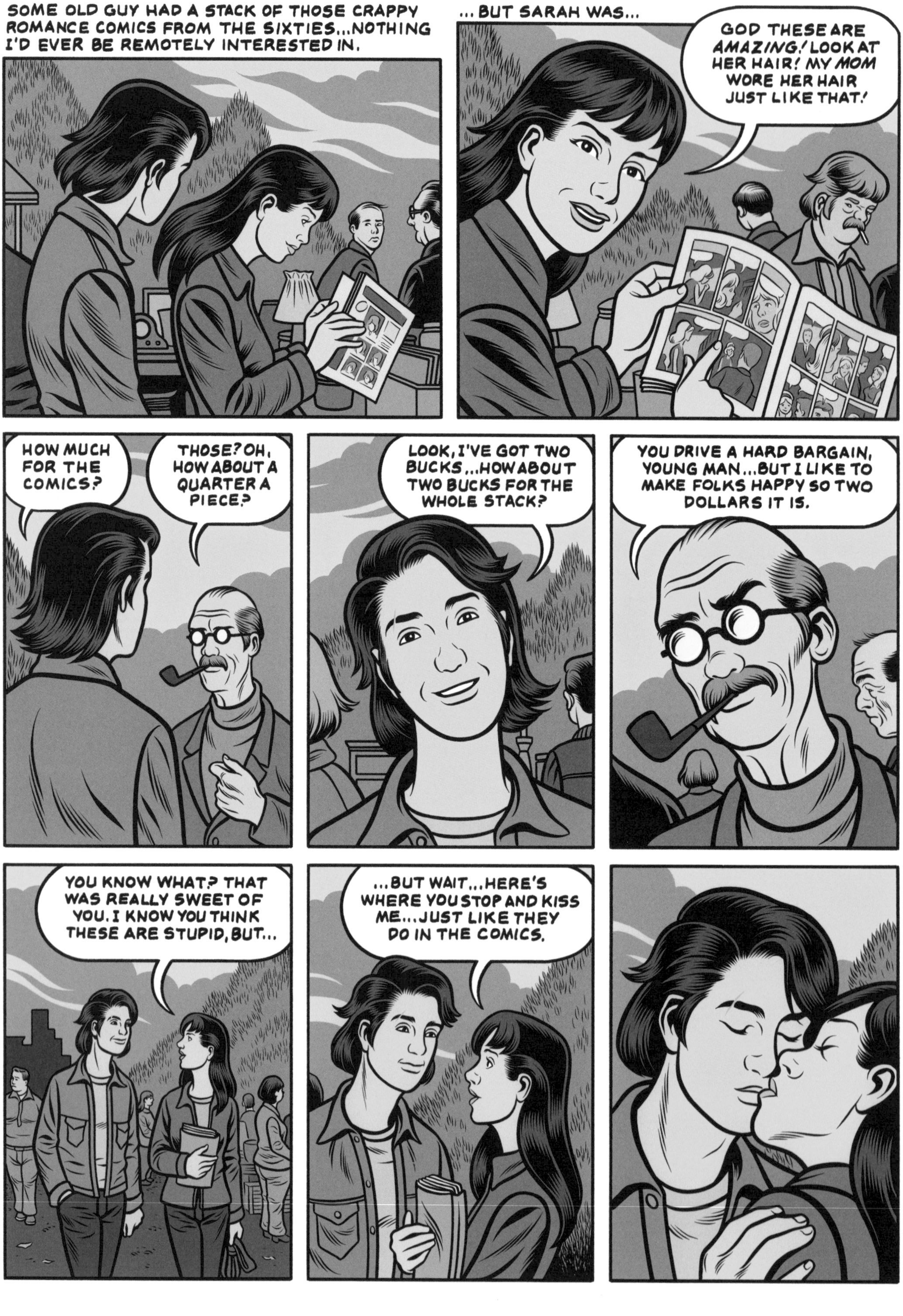
SOME OLD GUY HAD A STACK OF THOSE CRAPPY ROMANCE COMICS FROM THE SIXTIES...NOTHING I'D EVER BE REMOTELY INTERESTED IN.
... BUT SARAH WAS...
GOD THESE ARE AMAZING! LOOK AT HER HAIR! MY MOM WORE HER HAIR JUST LIKE THAT!
HOW MUCH FOR THE COMICS?
THOSE? OH, HOW ABOUT A QUARTER A PIECE?
LOOK, I'VE GOT TWO BUCKS...HOW ABOUT TWO BUCKS FOR THE WHOLE STACK?
YOU DRIVE A HARD BARGAIN, YOUNG MAN...BUT I LIKE TO MAKE FOLKS HAPPY SO TWO DOLLARS IT IS.
YOU KNOW WHAT? THAT WAS REALLY SWEET OF YOU. I KNOW YOU THINK THESE ARE STUPID, BUT...
...BUT WAIT...HERE'S WHERE YOU STOP AND KISS ME...JUST LIKE THEY DO IN THE COMICS.

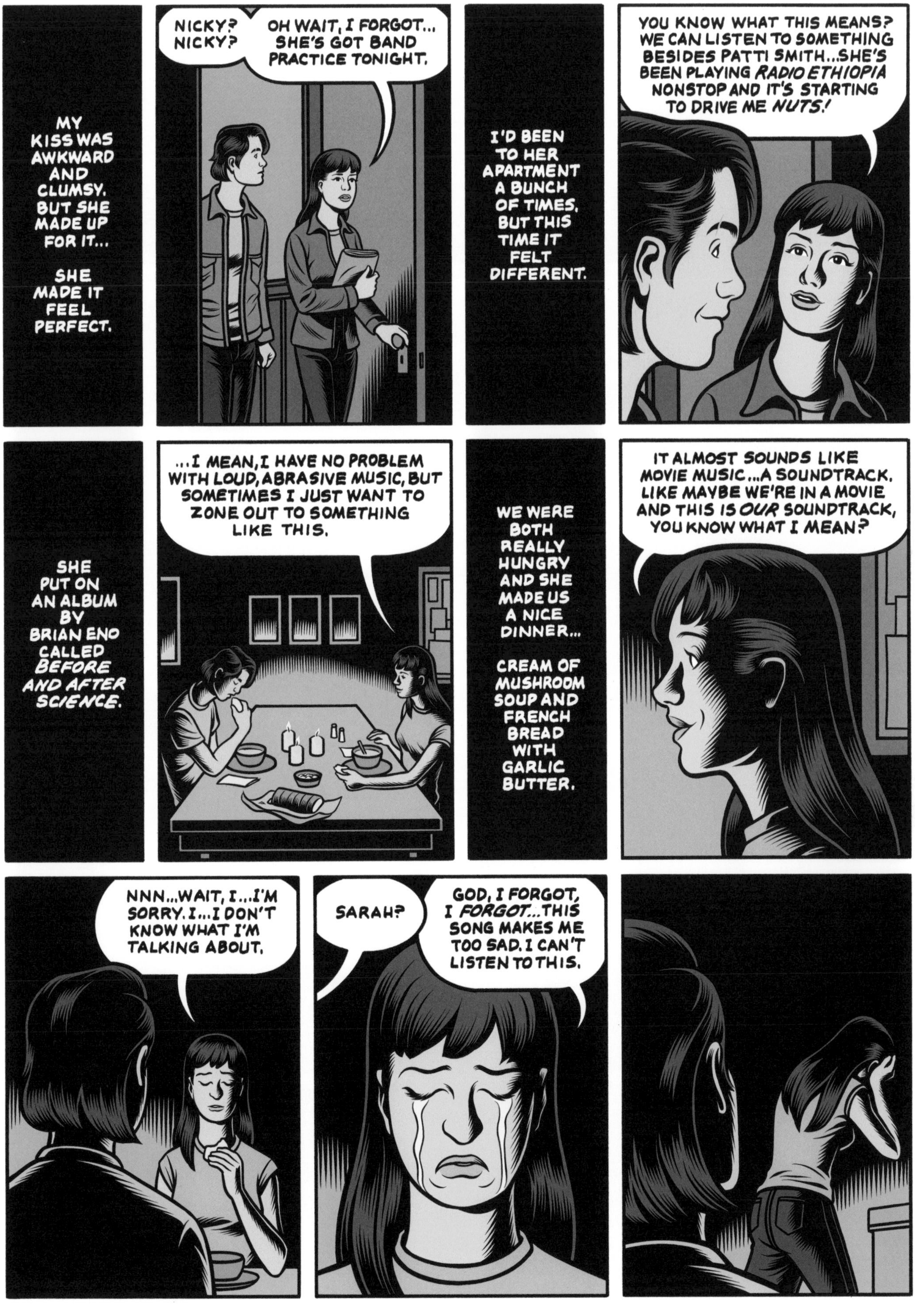
MY KISS WAS AWKWARD AND CLUMSY. BUT SHE MADE UP FOR IT...
SHE MADE IT FEEL PERFECT.
NICKY? NICKY?
OH WAIT, I FORGOT... SHE'S GOT BAND PRACTICE TONIGHT.
I'D BEEN TO HER APARTMENT A BUNCH OF TIMES, BUT THIS TIME IT FELT DIFFERENT.
YOU KNOW WHAT THIS MEANS? WE CAN LISTEN TO SOMETHING BESIDES PATTI SMITH...SHE'S BEEN PLAYING RADIO ETHIOPIA NONSTOP AND IT'S STARTING TO DRIVE ME NUTS!
SHE PUT ON AN ALBUM BY BRIAN ENO CALLED BEFORE AND AFTER SCIENCE.
...I MEAN, I HAVE NO PROBLEM WITH LOUD, ABRASIVE MUSIC, BUT SOMETIMES I JUST WANT TO ZONE OUT TO SOMETHING LIKE THIS.
WE WERE BOTH REALLY HUNGRY AND SHE MADE US A NICE DINNER...
CREAM OF MUSHROOM SOUP AND FRENCH BREAD WITH GARLIC BUTTER.
IT ALMOST SOUNDS LIKE MOVIE MUSIC...A SOUNDTRACK. LIKE MAYBE WE'RE IN A MOVIE AND THIS IS OUR SOUNDTRACK, YOU KNOW WHAT I MEAN?
NNN...WAIT, I...I'M SORRY. I...I DON'T KNOW WHAT I'M TALKING ABOUT.
SARAH?
GOD, I FORGOT, I FORGOT...THIS SONG MAKES ME TOO SAD. I CAN'T LISTEN TO THIS.

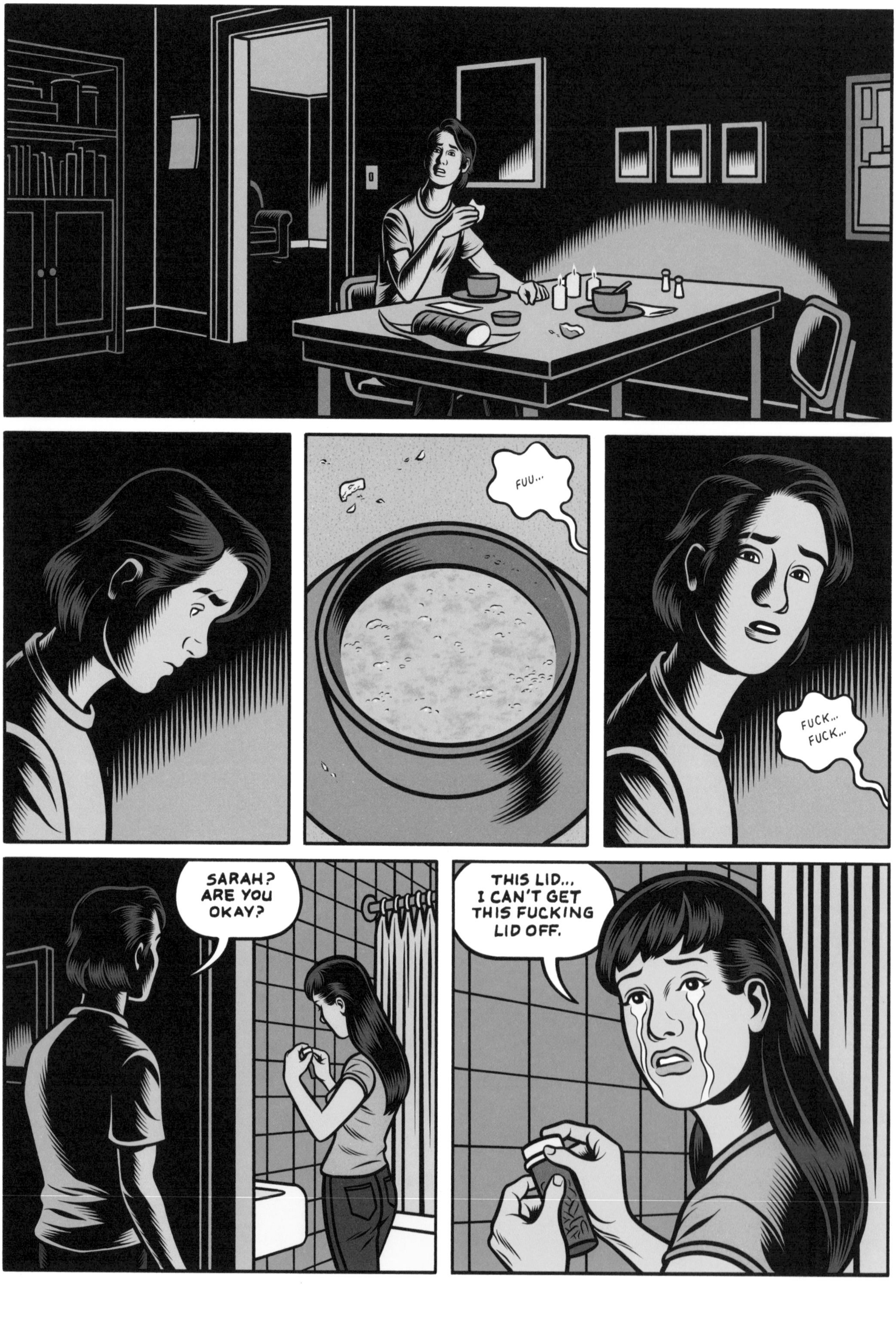
FUU...
FUCK... FUCK...
SARAH? ARE YOU OKAY?
THIS LID... I CAN'T GET THIS FUCKING LID OFF.

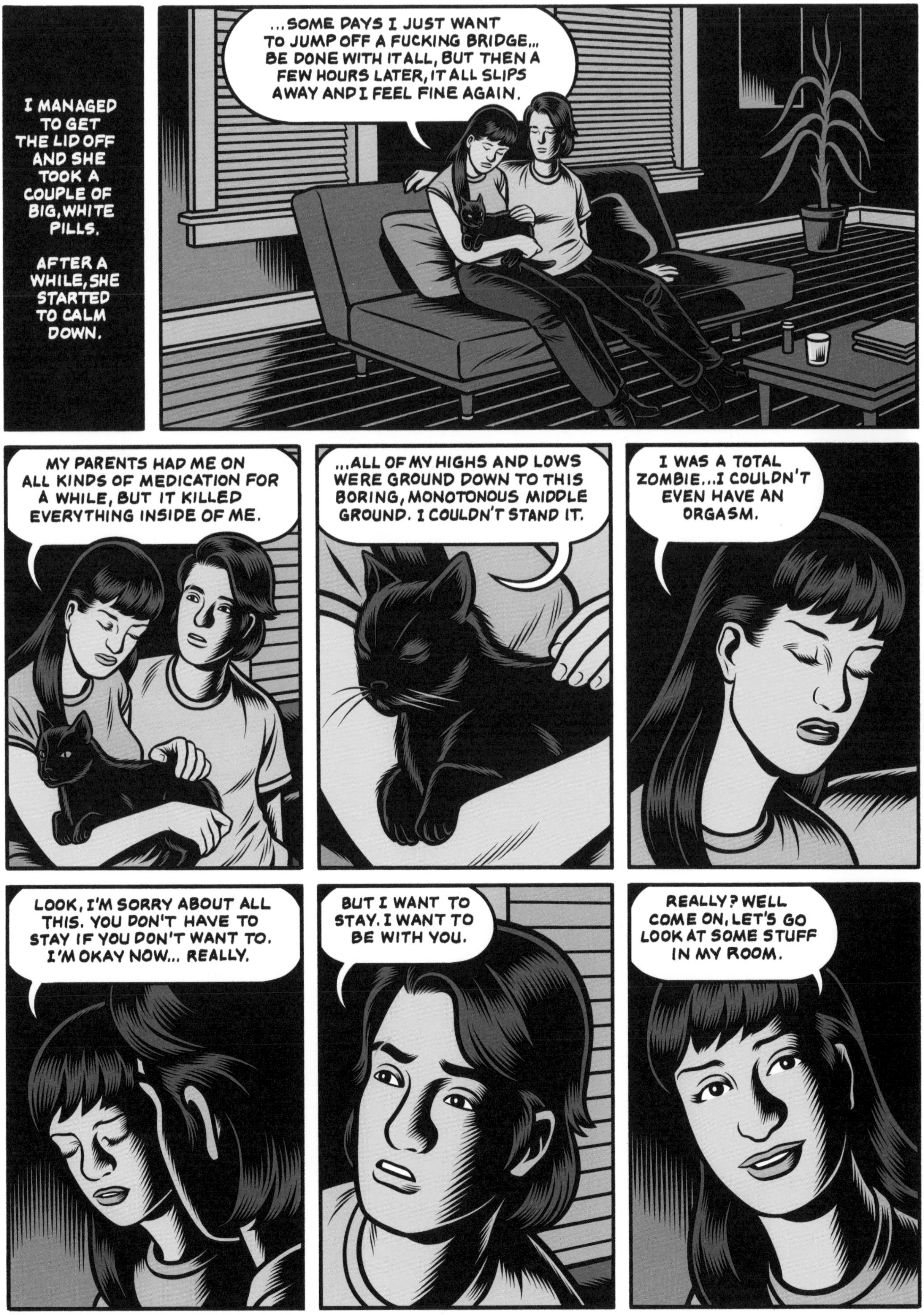
I MANAGED TO GET THE LID OFF AND SHE TOOK A COUPLE OF BIG, WHITE PILLS.
AFTER A WHILE, SHE STARTED TO CALM DOWN.
...SOME DAYS I JUST WANT TO JUMP OFF A FUCKING BRIDGE... BE DONE WITH IT ALL, BUT THEN A FEW HOURS LATER, IT ALL SLIPS AWAY AND I FEEL FINE AGAIN.
MY PARENTS HAD ME ON ALL KINDS OF MEDICATION FOR A WHILE, BUT IT KILLED EVERYTHING INSIDE OF ME.
...ALL OF MY HIGHS AND LOWS WERE GROUND DOWN TO THIS BORING, MONOTONOUS MIDDLE GROUND. I COULDN'T STAND IT.
I WAS A TOTAL ZOMBIE...I COULDN'T EVEN HAVE AN ORGASM.
LOOK, I'M SORRY ABOUT ALL THIS. YOU DON'T HAVE TO STAY IF YOU DON'T WANT TO. I'M OKAY NOW... REALLY.
BUT I WANT TO STAY. I WANT TO BE WITH YOU.
REALLY? WELL COME ON, LET'S GO LOOK AT SOME STUFF IN MY ROOM.

o safer.
d has no
n is like
That is,
TENSE NERVOUS
WOW. THESE ARE AMAZING.

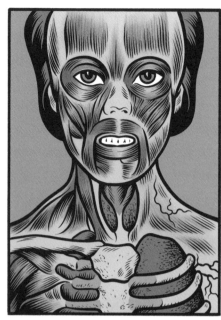

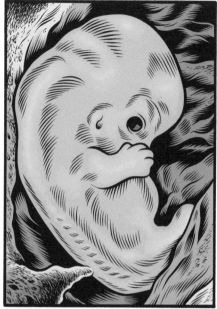

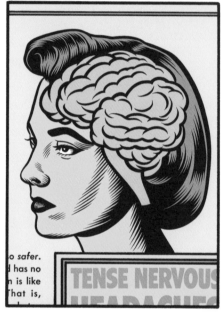

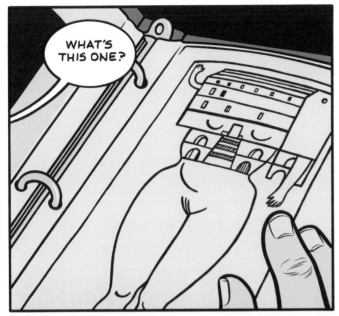

WHAT'S THIS ONE?

THAT'S BY LOUISE BOURGEOIS...SHE'S THIS AMAZING SCULPTOR, BUT THAT'S A DRAWING SHE DID BACK IN THE FORTIES WHEN SHE WAS RAISING A FAMILY.

IT'S CALLED FEMME MAISON. THE ENGLISH TRANSLATION WOULD BE HOUSE WOMAN OR HOUSEWIFE.

...SO YOU'VE GOT THIS BIG NAKED, ANONYMOUS WOMAN WITH A HOUSE FOR A HEAD...

...BUT WHAT'S SHE THINKING IN THERE? DOES SHE FEEL SAFE AND SECURE?

...OR DOES SHE FEEL TRAPPED?

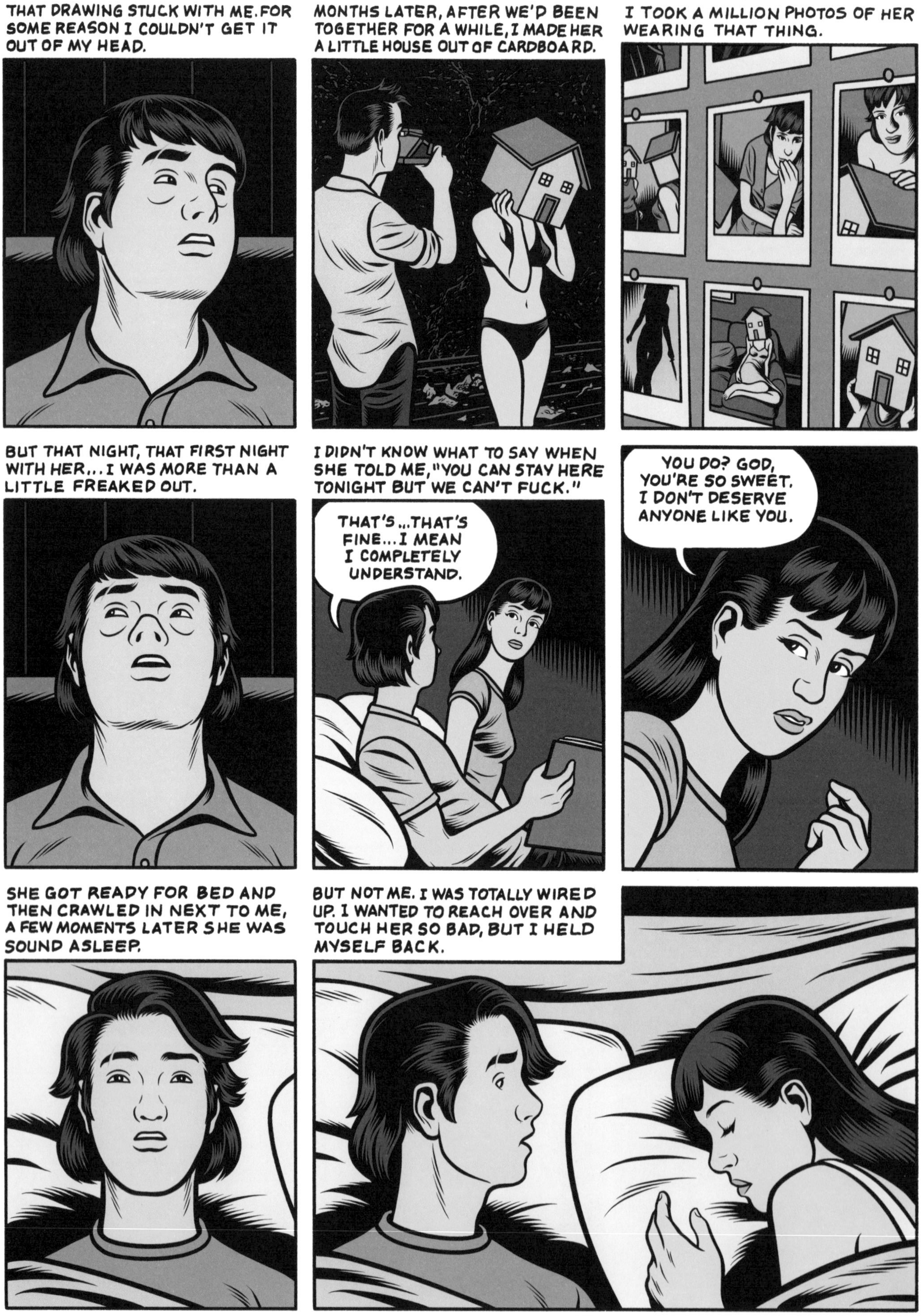

THAT DRAWING STUCK WITH ME. FOR SOME REASON I COULDN'T GET IT OUT OF MY HEAD.
MONTHS LATER, AFTER WE'D BEEN TOGETHER FOR A WHILE, I MADE HER A LITTLE HOUSE OUT OF CARDBOARD.
I TOOK A MILLION PHOTOS OF HER WEARING THAT THING.
BUT THAT NIGHT, THAT FIRST NIGHT WITH HER... I WAS MORE THAN A LITTLE FREAKED OUT.
I DIDN'T KNOW WHAT TO SAY WHEN SHE TOLD ME, "YOU CAN STAY HERE TONIGHT BUT WE CAN'T FUCK."
THAT'S...THAT'S FINE...I MEAN I COMPLETELY UNDERSTAND.
YOU DO? GOD, YOU'RE SO SWEET. I DON'T DESERVE ANYONE LIKE YOU.
SHE GOT READY FOR BED AND THEN CRAWLED IN NEXT TO ME, A FEW MOMENTS LATER SHE WAS SOUND ASLEEP.
BUT NOT ME. I WAS TOTALLY WIRED UP. I WANTED TO REACH OVER AND TOUCH HER SO BAD, BUT I HELD MYSELF BACK.

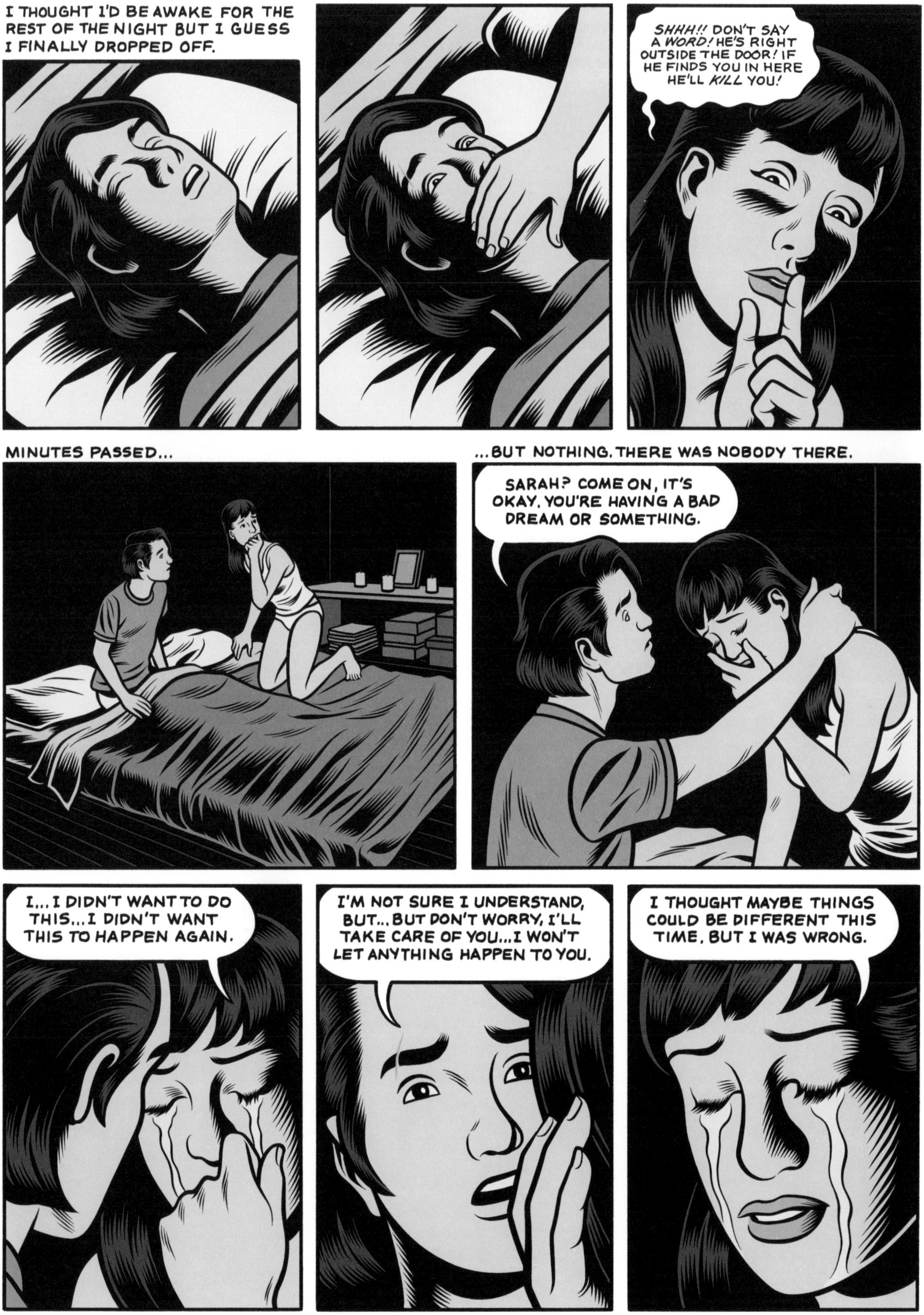
I THOUGHT I'D BE AWAKE FOR THE REST OF THE NIGHT BUT I GUESS I FINALLY DROPPED OFF.
SHHH!! DON'T SAY A WORD! HE'S RIGHT OUTSIDE THE DOOR! IF HE FINDS YOU IN HERE HE'LL KILL YOU!
MINUTES PASSED...
...BUT NOTHING. THERE WAS NOBODY THERE.
SARAH? COME ON, IT'S OKAY. YOU'RE HAVING A BAD DREAM OR SOMETHING.
I... I DIDN'T WANT TO DO THIS... I DIDN'T WANT THIS TO HAPPEN AGAIN.
I'M NOT SURE I UNDERSTAND, BUT... BUT DON'T WORRY, I'LL TAKE CARE OF YOU... I WON'T LET ANYTHING HAPPEN TO YOU.
I THOUGHT MAYBE THINGS COULD BE DIFFERENT THIS TIME, BUT I WAS WRONG.

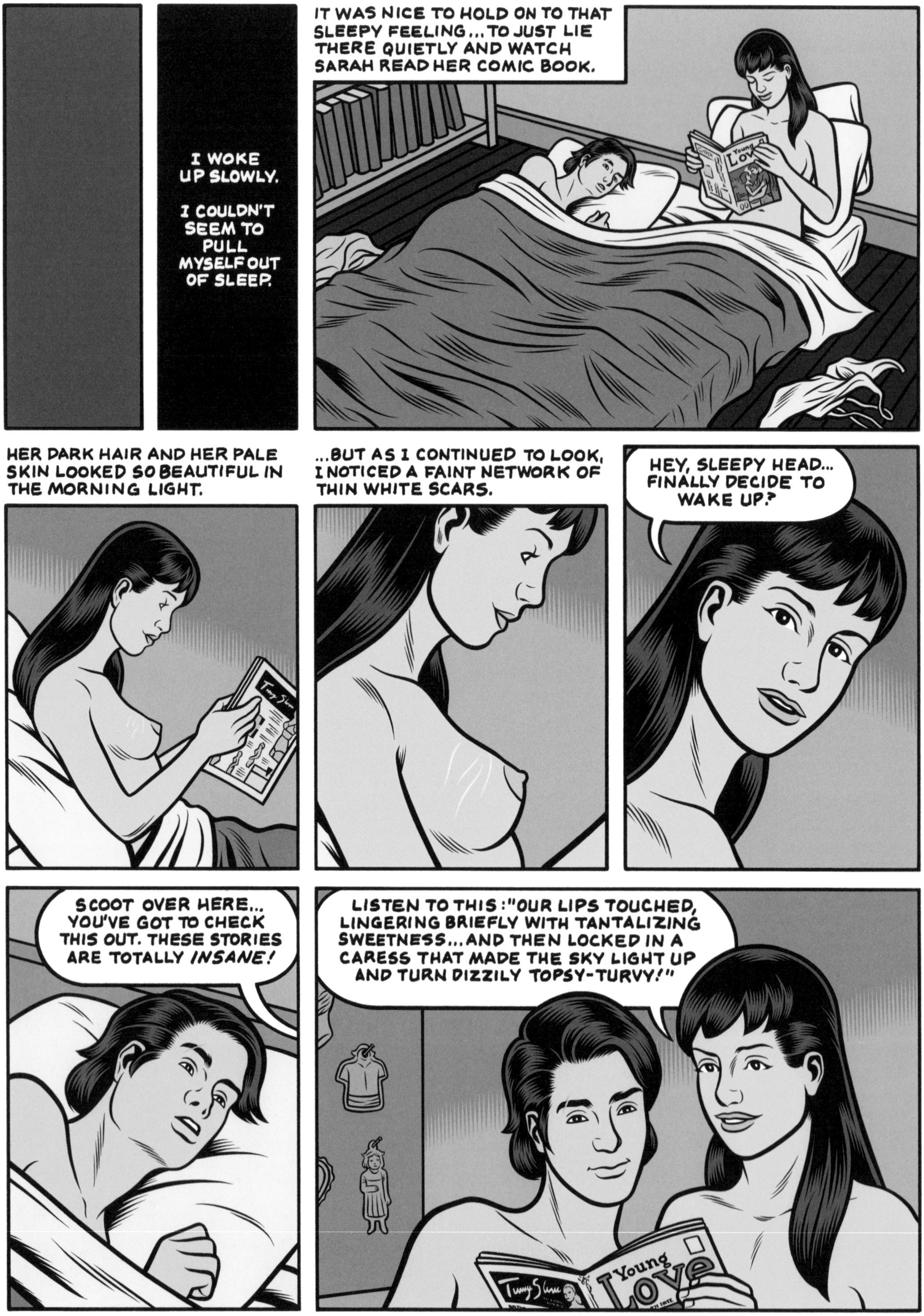
I WOKE UP SLOWLY.
I COULDN'T SEEM TO PULL MYSELF OUT OF SLEEP.
IT WAS NICE TO HOLD ON TO THAT SLEEPY FEELING... TO JUST LIE THERE QUIETLY AND WATCH SARAH READ HER COMIC BOOK.
Young Love
HER DARK HAIR AND HER PALE SKIN LOOKED SO BEAUTIFUL IN THE MORNING LIGHT.
...BUT AS I CONTINUED TO LOOK, I NOTICED A FAINT NETWORK OF THIN WHITE SCARS.
HEY, SLEEPY HEAD... FINALLY DECIDE TO WAKE UP?
SCOOT OVER HERE... YOU'VE GOT TO CHECK THIS OUT. THESE STORIES ARE TOTALLY *INSANE!*
LISTEN TO THIS: "OUR LIPS TOUCHED, LINGERING BRIEFLY WITH TANTALIZING SWEETNESS... AND THEN LOCKED IN A CARESS THAT MADE THE SKY LIGHT UP AND TURN DIZZILY TOPSY-TURVY!"
Young Love

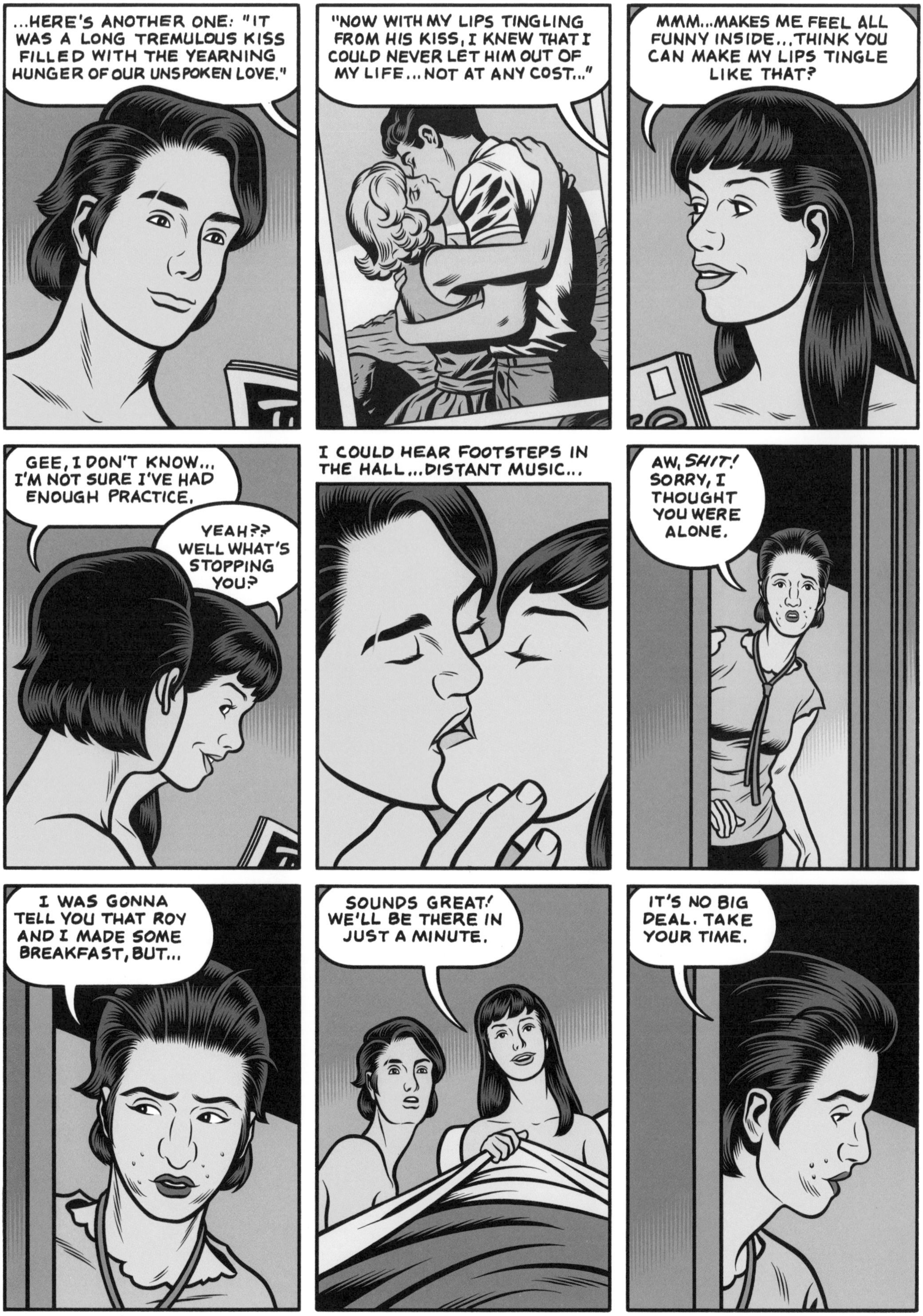
...HERE'S ANOTHER ONE: "IT WAS A LONG TREMULOUS KISS FILLED WITH THE YEARNING HUNGER OF OUR UNSPOKEN LOVE."
"NOW WITH MY LIPS TINGLING FROM HIS KISS, I KNEW THAT I COULD NEVER LET HIM OUT OF MY LIFE... NOT AT ANY COST..."
MMM...MAKES ME FEEL ALL FUNNY INSIDE... THINK YOU CAN MAKE MY LIPS TINGLE LIKE THAT?
GEE, I DON'T KNOW... I'M NOT SURE I'VE HAD ENOUGH PRACTICE.
YEAH?? WELL WHAT'S STOPPING YOU?
I COULD HEAR FOOTSTEPS IN THE HALL... DISTANT MUSIC...
AW, SHIT! SORRY, I THOUGHT YOU WERE ALONE.
I WAS GONNA TELL YOU THAT ROY AND I MADE SOME BREAKFAST, BUT...
SOUNDS GREAT! WE'LL BE THERE IN JUST A MINUTE.
IT'S NO BIG DEAL. TAKE YOUR TIME.

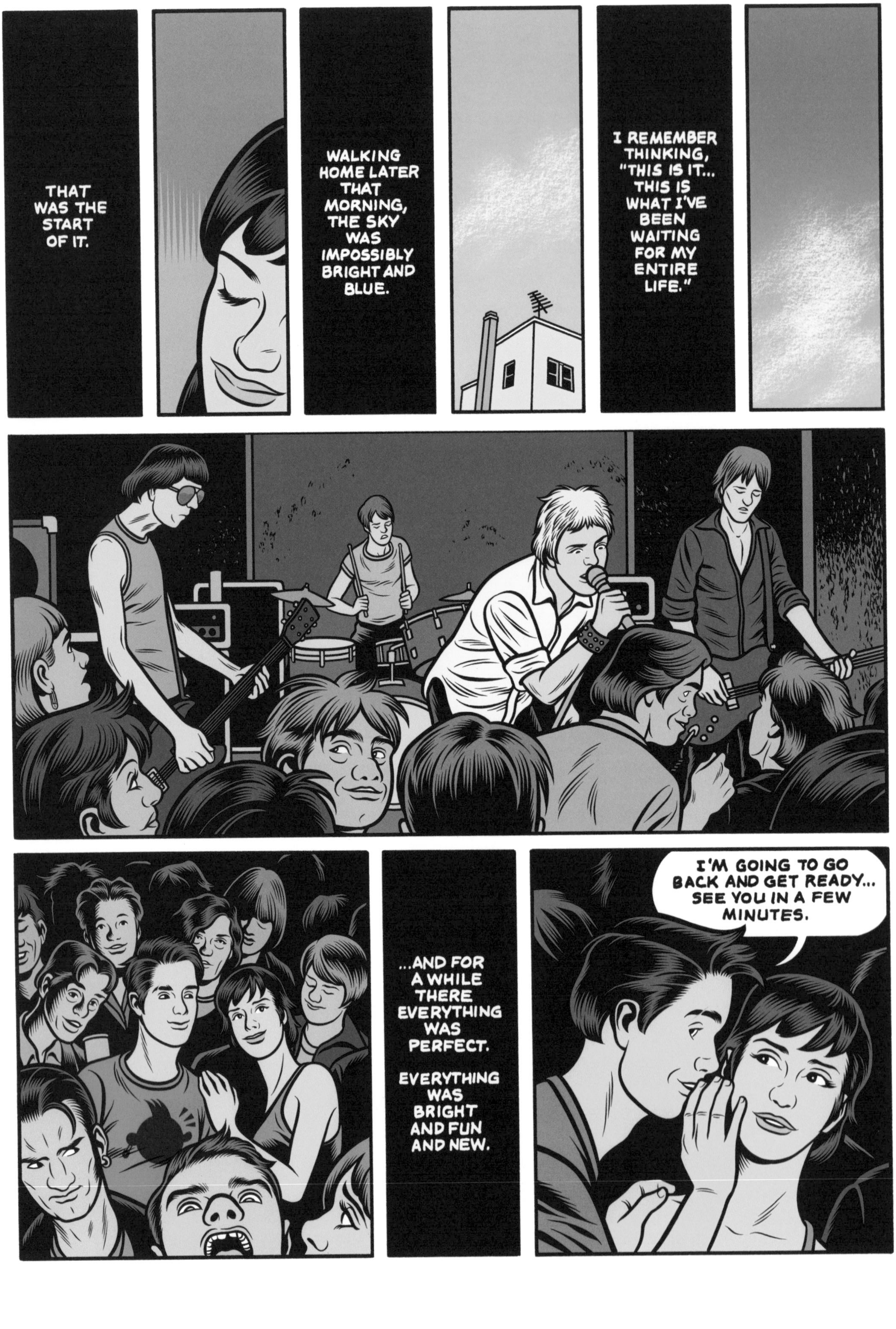

THAT WAS THE START OF IT.
WALKING HOME LATER THAT MORNING, THE SKY WAS IMPOSSIBLY BRIGHT AND BLUE.
I REMEMBER THINKING, "THIS IS IT... THIS IS WHAT I'VE BEEN WAITING FOR MY ENTIRE LIFE."
...AND FOR A WHILE THERE EVERYTHING WAS PERFECT.
EVERYTHING WAS BRIGHT AND FUN AND NEW.
I'M GOING TO GO BACK AND GET READY... SEE YOU IN A FEW MINUTES.

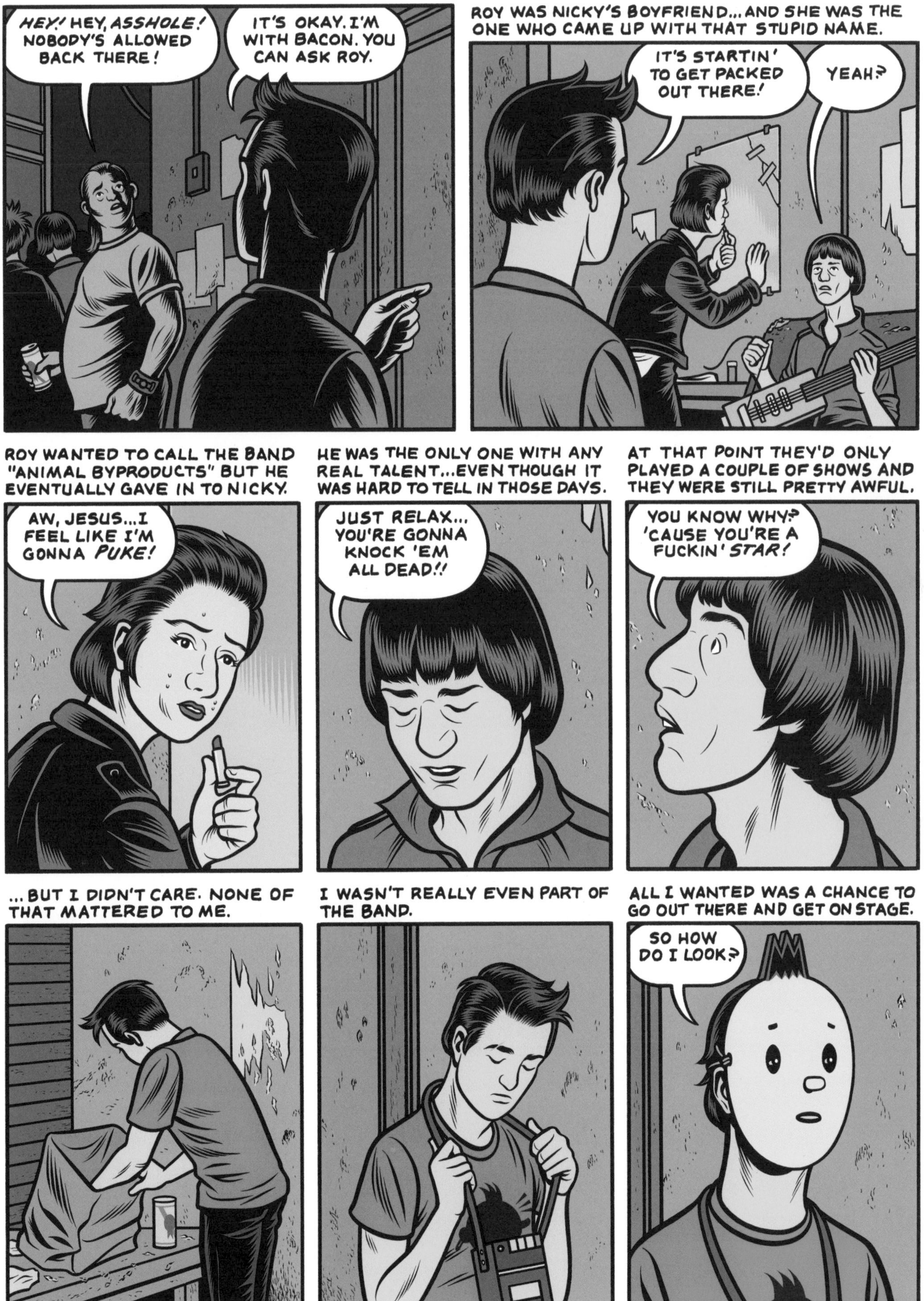
HEY! HEY, ASSHOLE! NOBODY'S ALLOWED BACK THERE!
IT'S OKAY. I'M WITH BACON. YOU CAN ASK ROY.
ROY WAS NICKY'S BOYFRIEND... AND SHE WAS THE ONE WHO CAME UP WITH THAT STUPID NAME.
IT'S STARTIN' TO GET PACKED OUT THERE!
YEAH?
ROY WANTED TO CALL THE BAND "ANIMAL BYPRODUCTS" BUT HE EVENTUALLY GAVE IN TO NICKY.
AW, JESUS...I FEEL LIKE I'M GONNA PUKE!
HE WAS THE ONLY ONE WITH ANY REAL TALENT... EVEN THOUGH IT WAS HARD TO TELL IN THOSE DAYS.
JUST RELAX... YOU'RE GONNA KNOCK 'EM ALL DEAD!!
AT THAT POINT THEY'D ONLY PLAYED A COUPLE OF SHOWS AND THEY WERE STILL PRETTY AWFUL.
YOU KNOW WHY? 'CAUSE YOU'RE A FUCKIN' STAR!
... BUT I DIDN'T CARE. NONE OF THAT MATTERED TO ME.
I WASN'T REALLY EVEN PART OF THE BAND.
ALL I WANTED WAS A CHANCE TO GO OUT THERE AND GET ON STAGE.
SO HOW DO I LOOK?

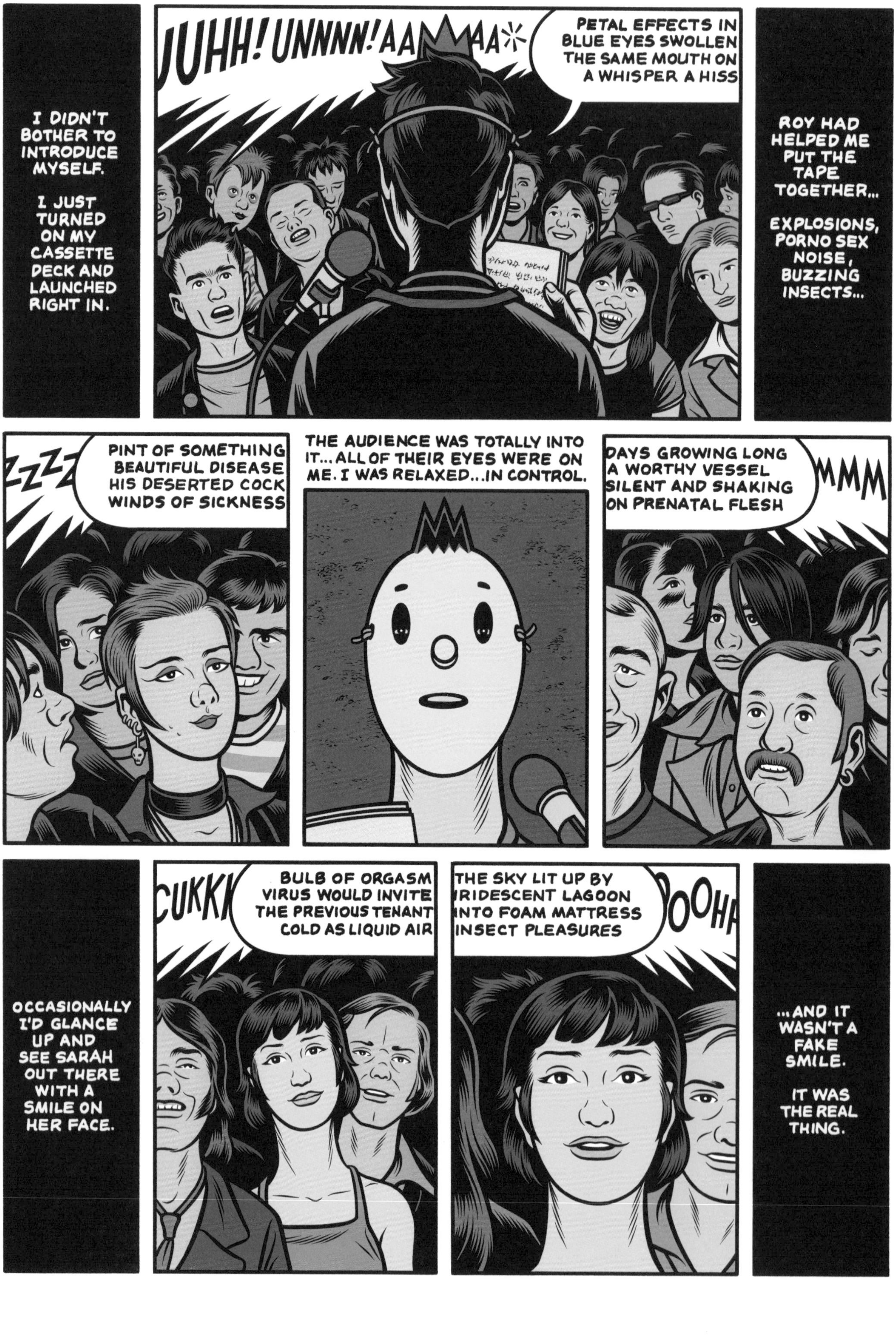
I DIDN'T BOTHER TO INTRODUCE MYSELF.
I JUST TURNED ON MY CASSETTE DECK AND LAUNCHED RIGHT IN.
UUHH! UNNNN! AA AA
PETAL EFFECTS IN BLUE EYES SWOLLEN THE SAME MOUTH ON A WHISPER A HISS
ROY HAD HELPED ME PUT THE TAPE TOGETHER...
EXPLOSIONS, PORNO SEX NOISE, BUZZING INSECTS...
ZZZZ
PINT OF SOMETHING BEAUTIFUL DISEASE HIS DESERTED COCK WINDS OF SICKNESS
THE AUDIENCE WAS TOTALLY INTO IT... ALL OF THEIR EYES WERE ON ME. I WAS RELAXED... IN CONTROL.
DAYS GROWING LONG A WORTHY VESSEL SILENT AND SHAKING ON PRENATAL FLESH
MMM
OCCASIONALLY I'D GLANCE UP AND SEE SARAH OUT THERE WITH A SMILE ON HER FACE.
CUKK
BULB OF ORGASM VIRUS WOULD INVITE THE PREVIOUS TENANT COLD AS LIQUID AIR
THE SKY LIT UP BY IRIDESCENT LAGOON INTO FOAM MATTRESS INSECT PLEASURES
OOHH
...AND IT WASN'T A FAKE SMILE.
IT WAS THE REAL THING.

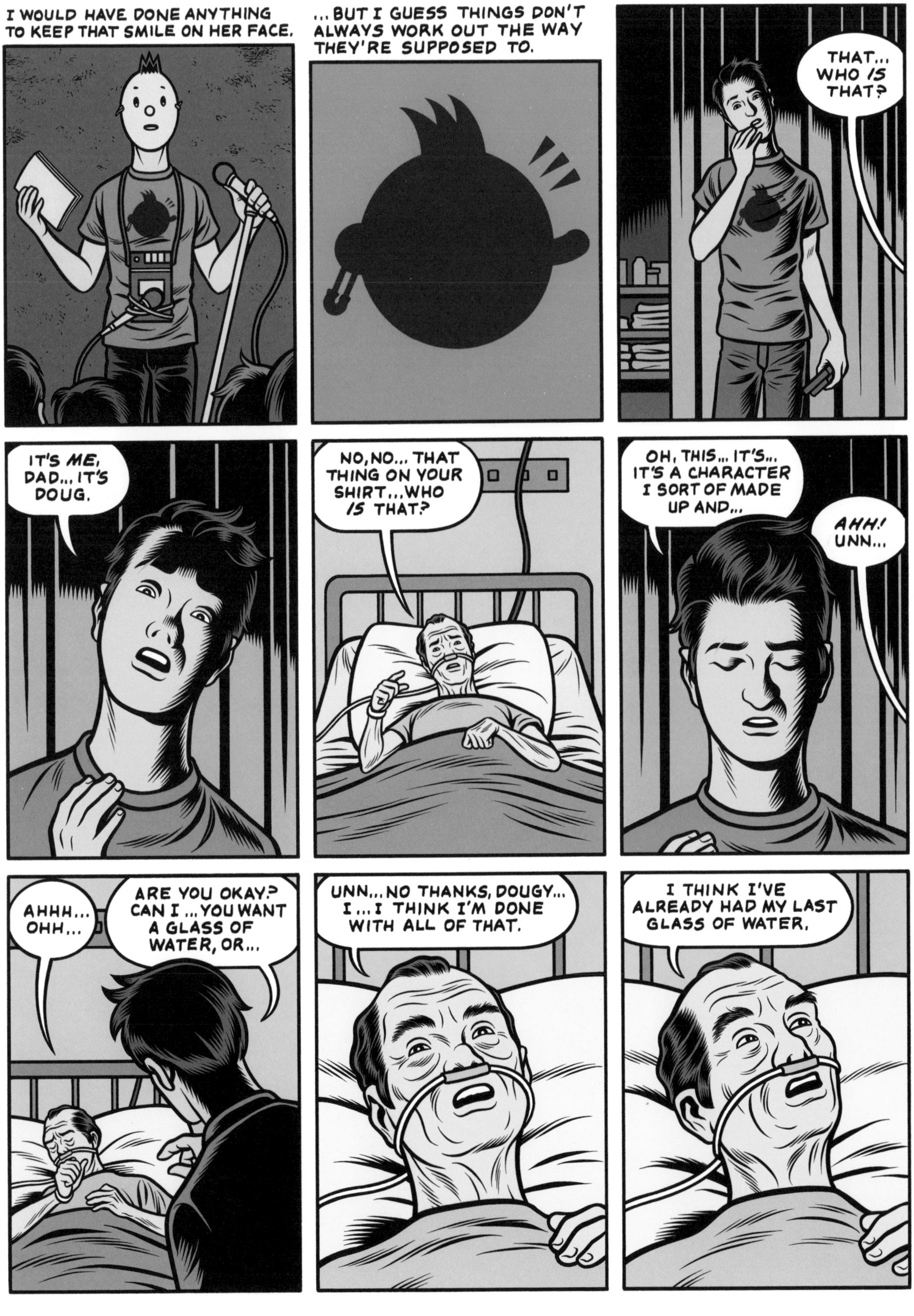
I WOULD HAVE DONE ANYTHING TO KEEP THAT SMILE ON HER FACE.
... BUT I GUESS THINGS DON'T ALWAYS WORK OUT THE WAY THEY'RE SUPPOSED TO.
THAT... WHO *IS* THAT?
IT'S *ME*, DAD... IT'S DOUG.
NO, NO... THAT THING ON YOUR SHIRT... WHO *IS* THAT?
OH, THIS... IT'S... IT'S A CHARACTER I SORT OF MADE UP AND...
*AHH!* UNN...
AHHH... OHH...
ARE YOU OKAY? CAN I ... YOU WANT A GLASS OF WATER, OR...
UNN... NO THANKS, DOUGY... I ... I THINK I'M DONE WITH ALL OF THAT.
I THINK I'VE ALREADY HAD MY LAST GLASS OF WATER.

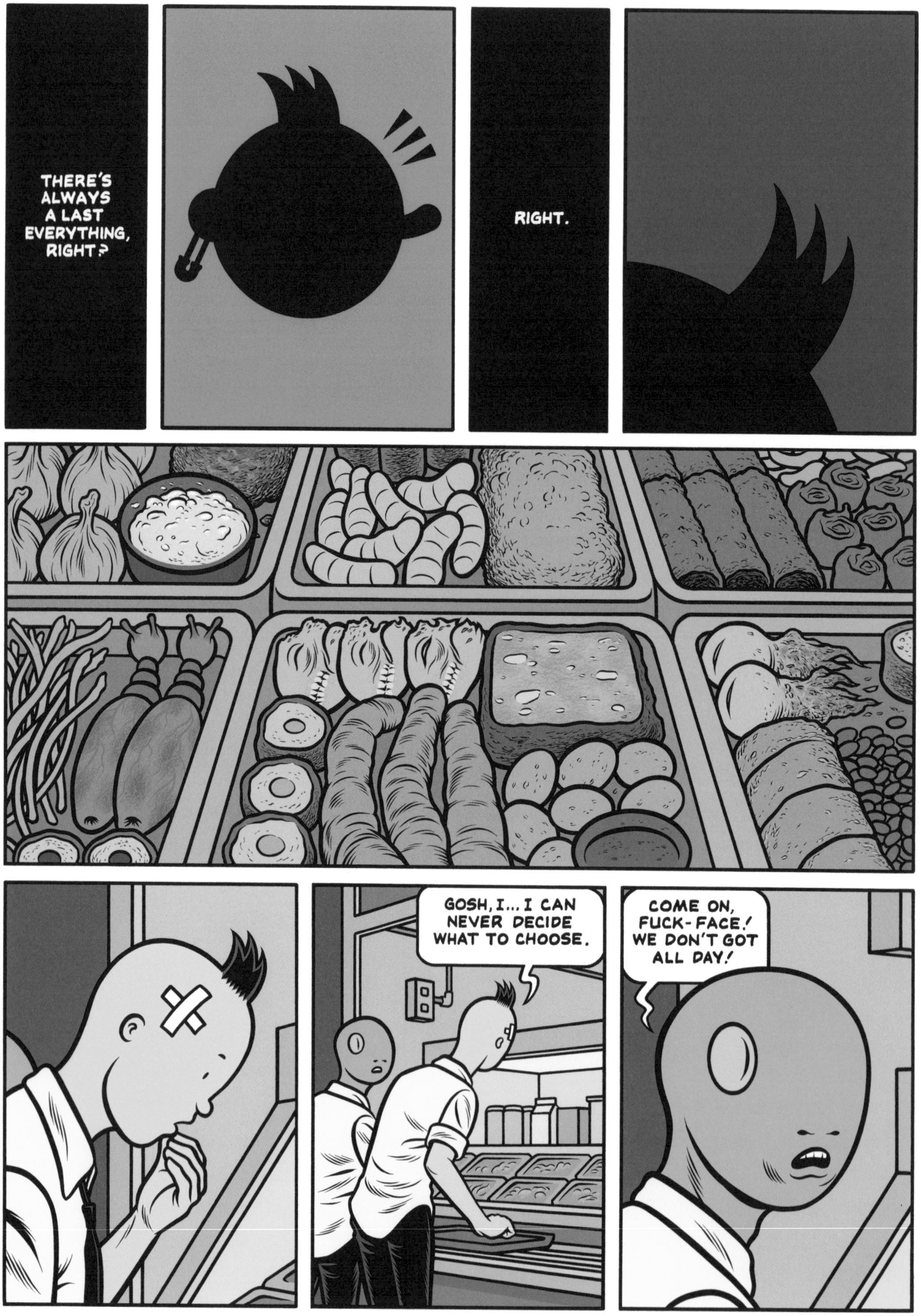
THERE'S ALWAYS A LAST EVERYTHING, RIGHT?
RIGHT.
GOSH, I... I CAN NEVER DECIDE WHAT TO CHOOSE.
COME ON, FUCK-FACE! WE DON'T GOT ALL DAY!

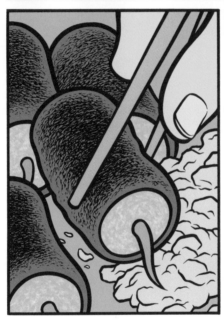

MMM...
LOOKS MIGHTY
TASTY.

HEY, HEY!
I THOUGHT
I MIGHT FIND
YOU HERE!

LOOK, I HATE TO SAY IT BUT
I'VE GOT A FEW UNANTICIPATED
EXPENSES THIS WEEK AND I'M
GONNA HAVE TO HIT YOU UP
FOR AN ADVANCE.

AN ADVANCE? DIDN'T I JUST
GIVE YOU AN ADVANCE A COUPLE
OF DAYS AGO?

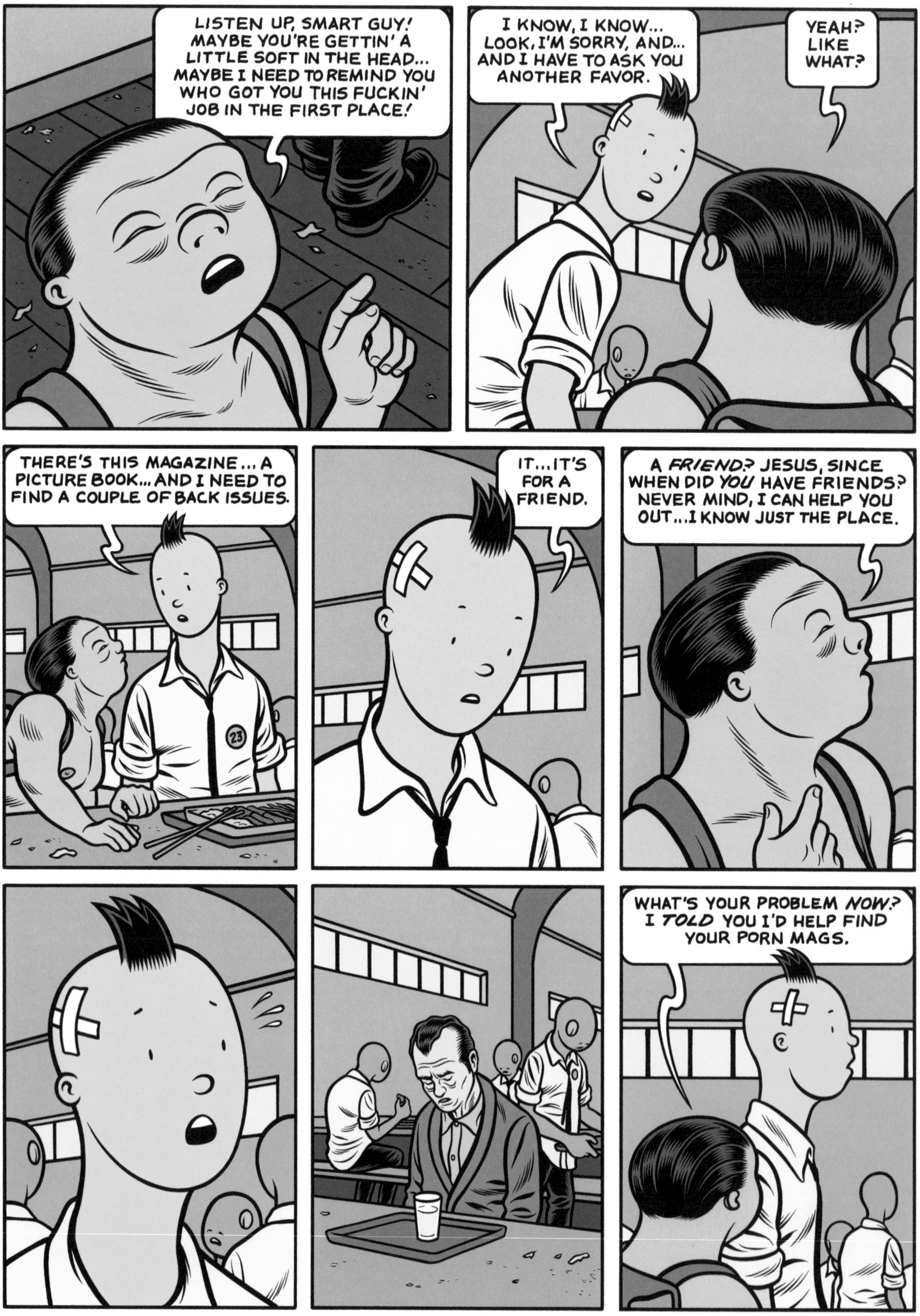
LISTEN UP, SMART GUY! MAYBE YOU'RE GETTIN' A LITTLE SOFT IN THE HEAD... MAYBE I NEED TO REMIND YOU WHO GOT YOU THIS FUCKIN' JOB IN THE FIRST PLACE!
I KNOW, I KNOW... LOOK, I'M SORRY, AND... AND I HAVE TO ASK YOU ANOTHER FAVOR.
YEAH? LIKE WHAT?
THERE'S THIS MAGAZINE... A PICTURE BOOK... AND I NEED TO FIND A COUPLE OF BACK ISSUES.
IT... IT'S FOR A FRIEND.
A FRIEND? JESUS, SINCE WHEN DID YOU HAVE FRIENDS? NEVER MIND, I CAN HELP YOU OUT... I KNOW JUST THE PLACE.
WHAT'S YOUR PROBLEM NOW? I TOLD YOU I'D HELP FIND YOUR PORN MAGS.

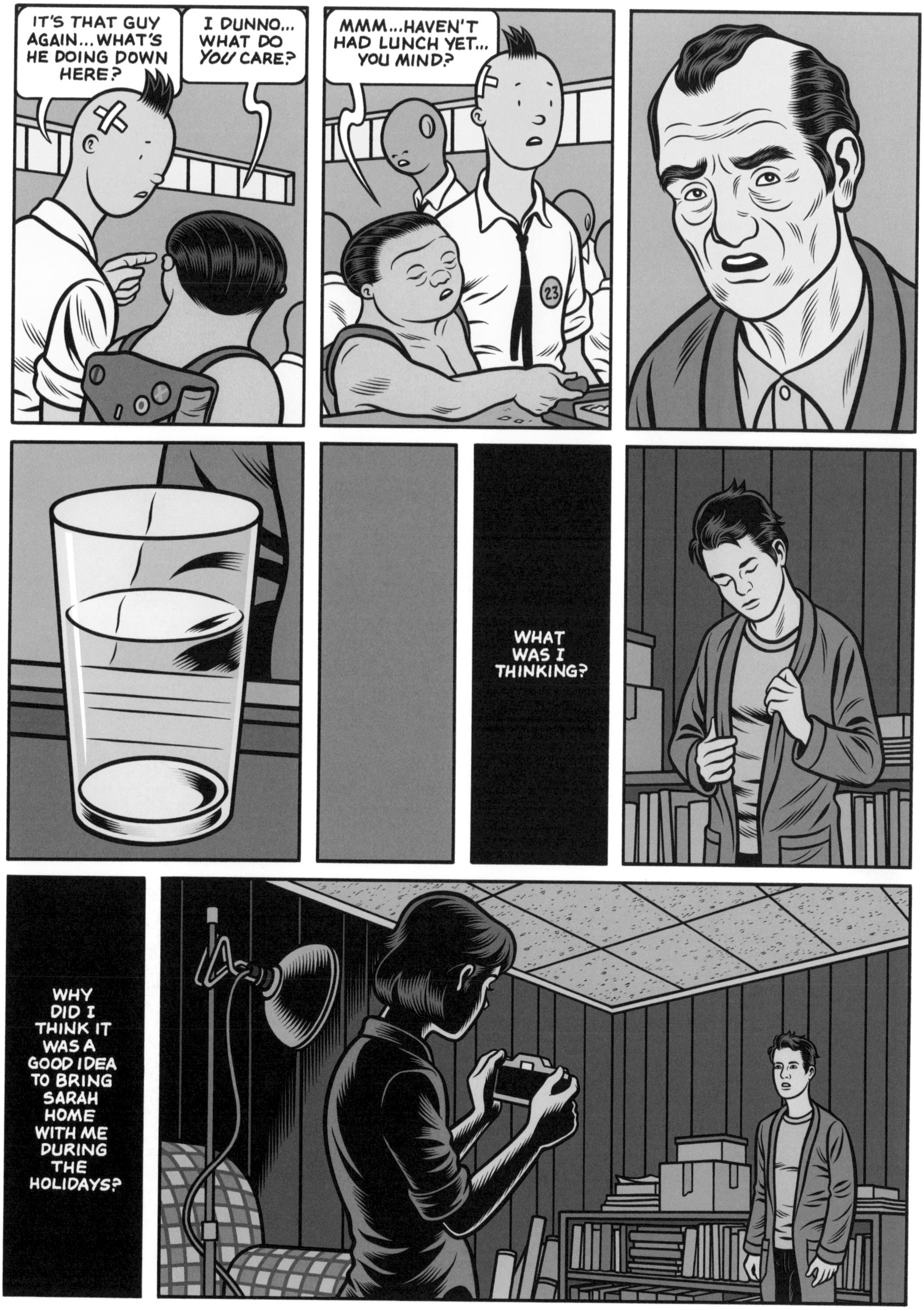
IT'S THAT GUY AGAIN... WHAT'S HE DOING DOWN HERE?
I DUNNO... WHAT DO *YOU* CARE?
MMM... HAVEN'T HAD LUNCH YET... YOU MIND?
23
WHAT WAS I THINKING?
WHY DID I THINK IT WAS A GOOD IDEA TO BRING SARAH HOME WITH ME DURING THE HOLIDAYS?

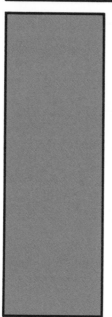

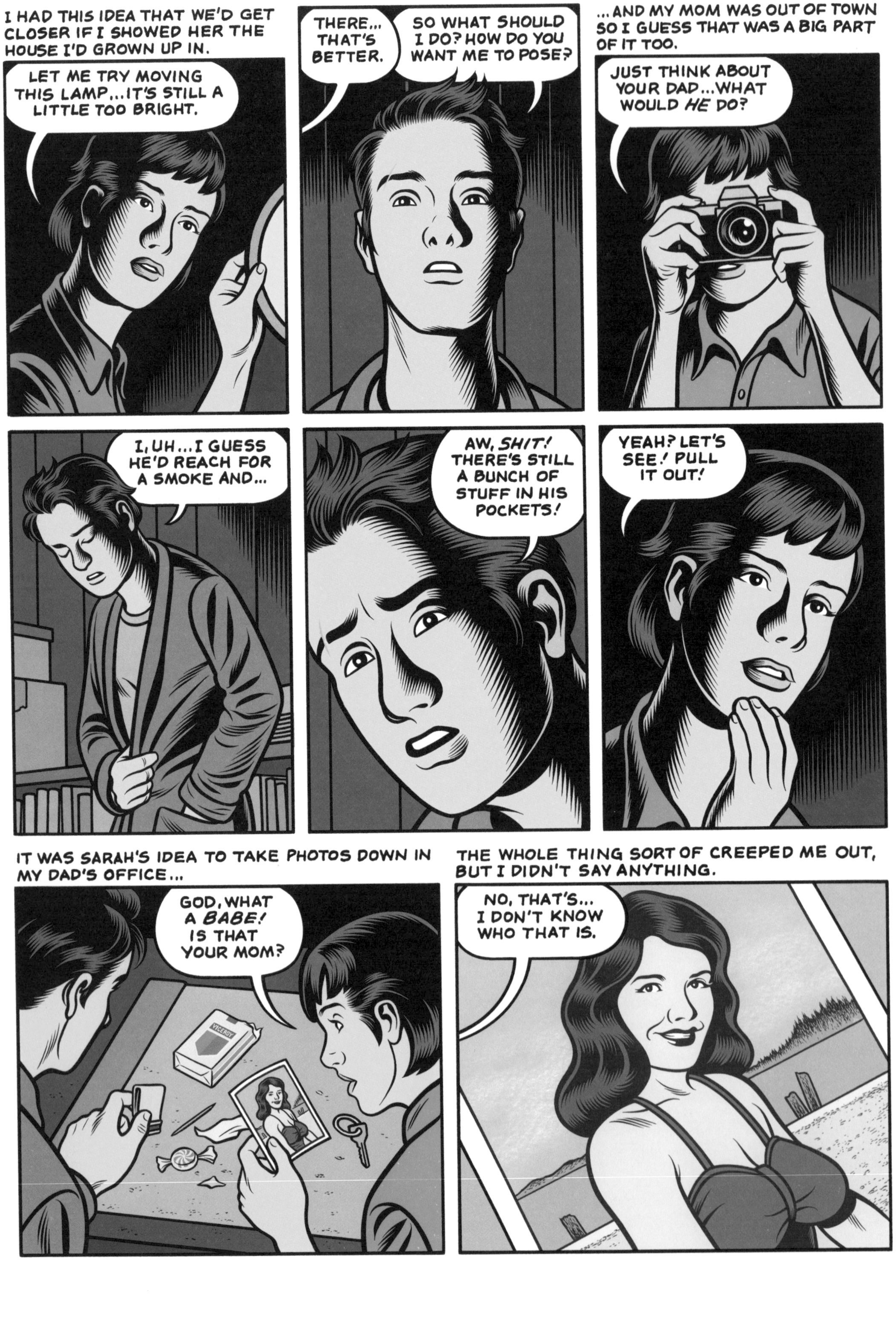
I HAD THIS IDEA THAT WE'D GET CLOSER IF I SHOWED HER THE HOUSE I'D GROWN UP IN.
LET ME TRY MOVING THIS LAMP,..IT'S STILL A LITTLE TOO BRIGHT.
THERE... THAT'S BETTER.
SO WHAT SHOULD I DO? HOW DO YOU WANT ME TO POSE?
...AND MY MOM WAS OUT OF TOWN SO I GUESS THAT WAS A BIG PART OF IT TOO.
JUST THINK ABOUT YOUR DAD...WHAT WOULD HE DO?
I, UH...I GUESS HE'D REACH FOR A SMOKE AND...
AW, SHIT! THERE'S STILL A BUNCH OF STUFF IN HIS POCKETS!
YEAH? LET'S SEE! PULL IT OUT!
IT WAS SARAH'S IDEA TO TAKE PHOTOS DOWN IN MY DAD'S OFFICE...
GOD, WHAT A BABE! IS THAT YOUR MOM?
VICEROY
THE WHOLE THING SORT OF CREEPED ME OUT, BUT I DIDN'T SAY ANYTHING.
NO, THAT'S... I DON'T KNOW WHO THAT IS.

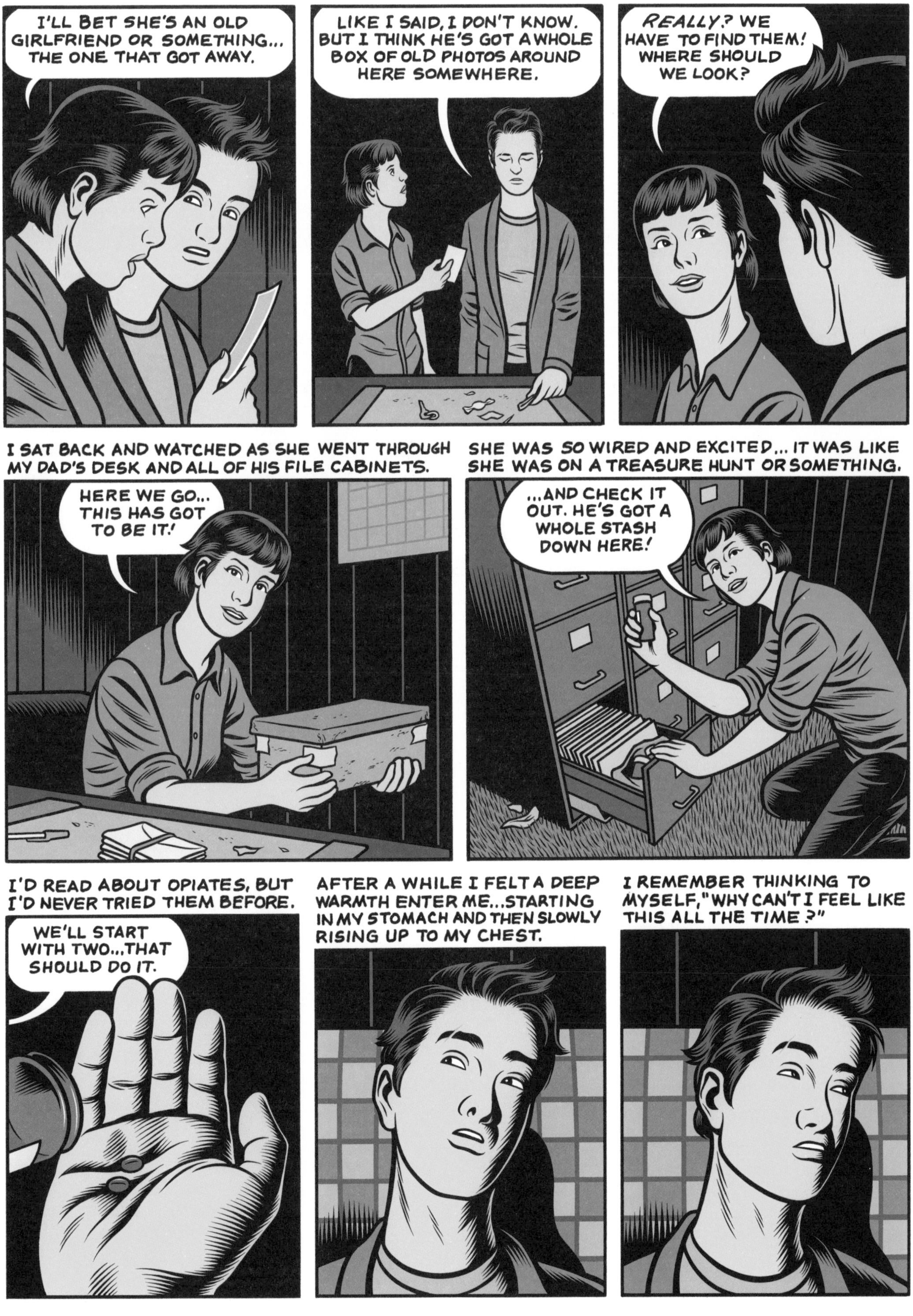
I'LL BET SHE'S AN OLD GIRLFRIEND OR SOMETHING... THE ONE THAT GOT AWAY.
LIKE I SAID, I DON'T KNOW. BUT I THINK HE'S GOT A WHOLE BOX OF OLD PHOTOS AROUND HERE SOMEWHERE.
REALLY? WE HAVE TO FIND THEM! WHERE SHOULD WE LOOK?
I SAT BACK AND WATCHED AS SHE WENT THROUGH MY DAD'S DESK AND ALL OF HIS FILE CABINETS.
HERE WE GO... THIS HAS GOT TO BE IT!
SHE WAS SO WIRED AND EXCITED... IT WAS LIKE SHE WAS ON A TREASURE HUNT OR SOMETHING.
...AND CHECK IT OUT. HE'S GOT A WHOLE STASH DOWN HERE!
I'D READ ABOUT OPIATES, BUT I'D NEVER TRIED THEM BEFORE.
WE'LL START WITH TWO... THAT SHOULD DO IT.
AFTER A WHILE I FELT A DEEP WARMTH ENTER ME... STARTING IN MY STOMACH AND THEN SLOWLY RISING UP TO MY CHEST.
I REMEMBER THINKING TO MYSELF, "WHY CAN'T I FEEL LIKE THIS ALL THE TIME?"

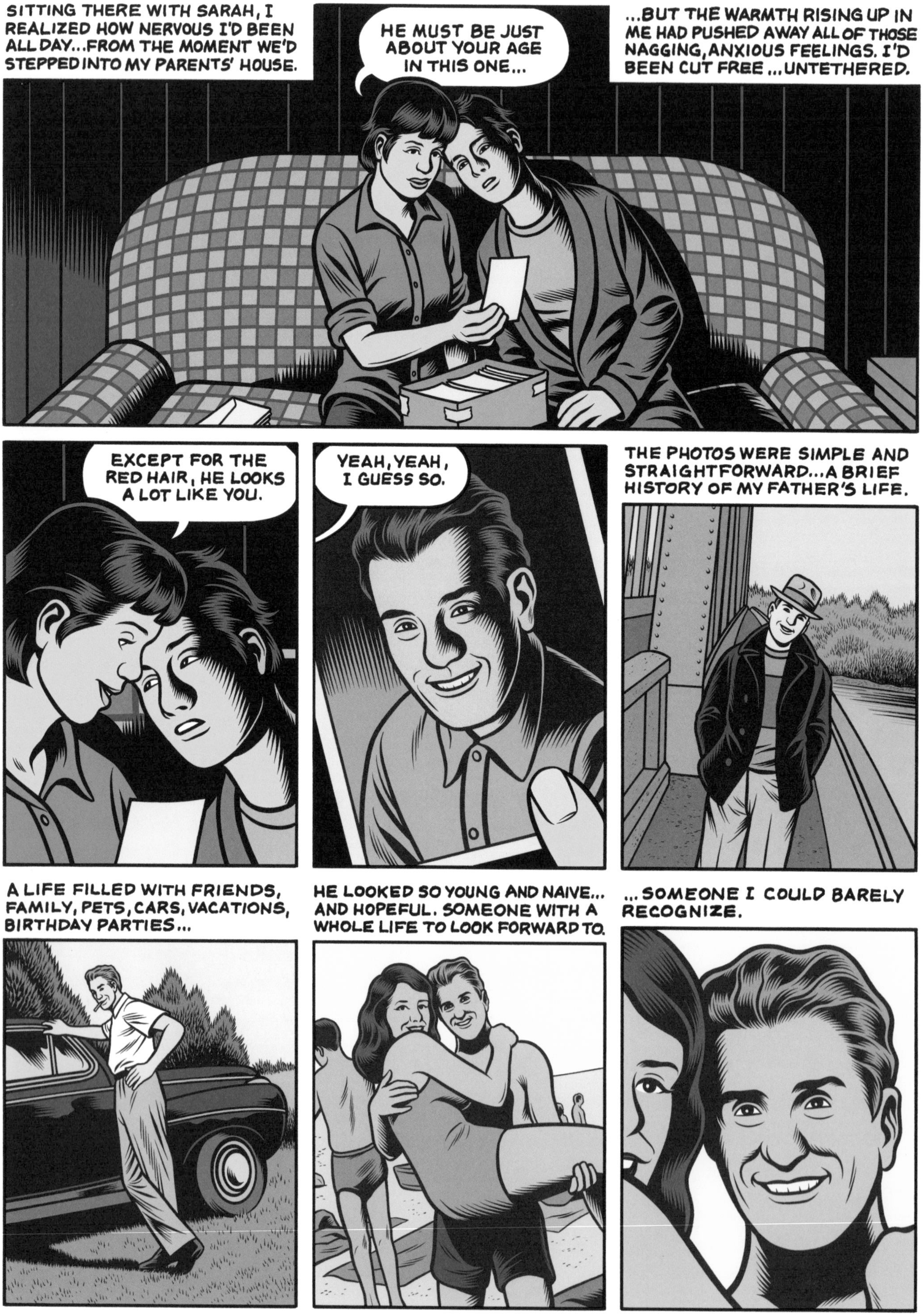
SITTING THERE WITH SARAH, I REALIZED HOW NERVOUS I'D BEEN ALL DAY... FROM THE MOMENT WE'D STEPPED INTO MY PARENTS' HOUSE.
HE MUST BE JUST ABOUT YOUR AGE IN THIS ONE...
...BUT THE WARMTH RISING UP IN ME HAD PUSHED AWAY ALL OF THOSE NAGGING, ANXIOUS FEELINGS. I'D BEEN CUT FREE ... UNTETHERED.
EXCEPT FOR THE RED HAIR, HE LOOKS A LOT LIKE YOU.
YEAH, YEAH, I GUESS SO.
THE PHOTOS WERE SIMPLE AND STRAIGHTFORWARD... A BRIEF HISTORY OF MY FATHER'S LIFE.
A LIFE FILLED WITH FRIENDS, FAMILY, PETS, CARS, VACATIONS, BIRTHDAY PARTIES...
HE LOOKED SO YOUNG AND NAIVE... AND HOPEFUL. SOMEONE WITH A WHOLE LIFE TO LOOK FORWARD TO.
... SOMEONE I COULD BARELY RECOGNIZE.

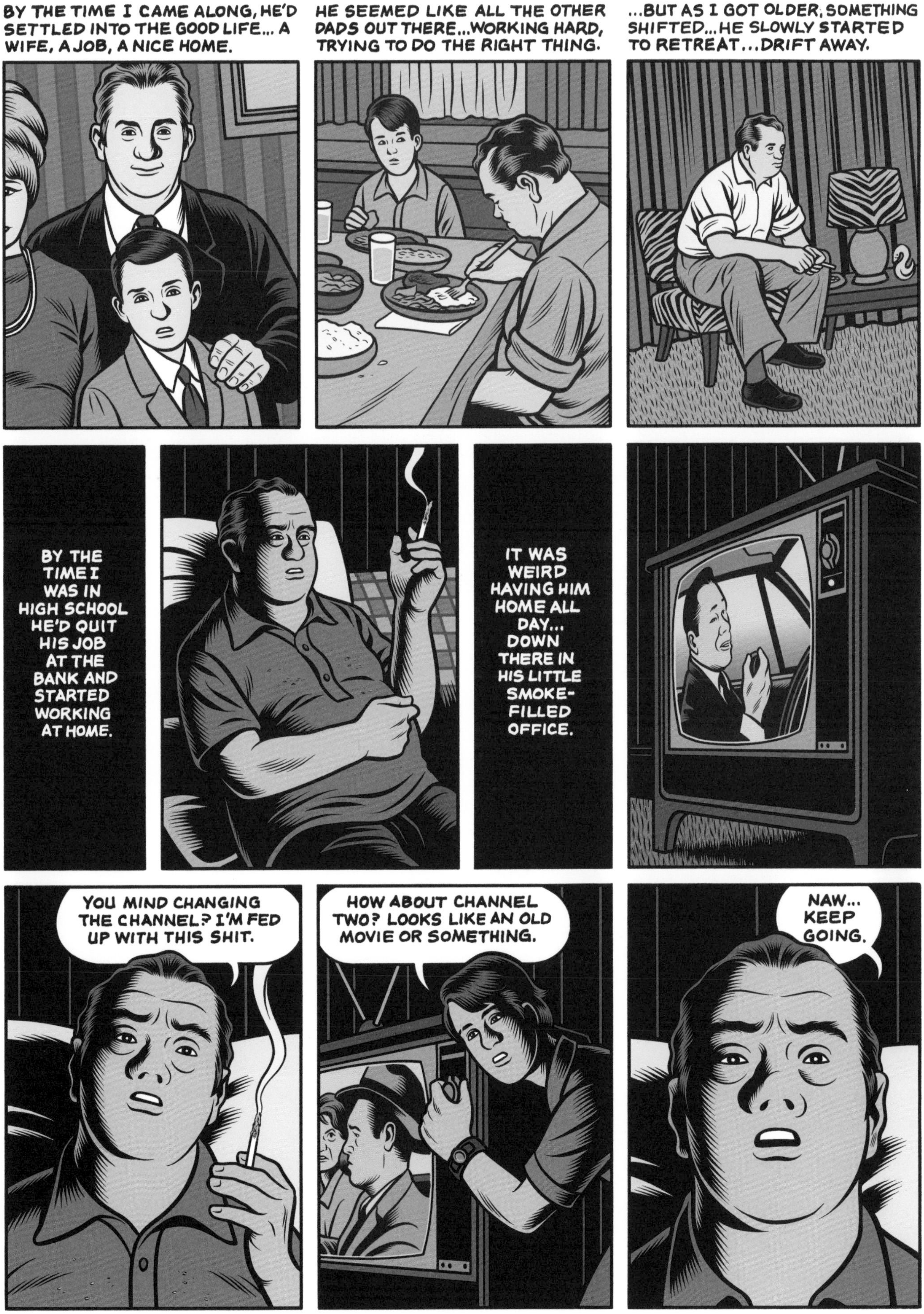

BY THE TIME I CAME ALONG, HE'D SETTLED INTO THE GOOD LIFE... A WIFE, A JOB, A NICE HOME.
HE SEEMED LIKE ALL THE OTHER DADS OUT THERE... WORKING HARD, TRYING TO DO THE RIGHT THING.
...BUT AS I GOT OLDER, SOMETHING SHIFTED... HE SLOWLY STARTED TO RETREAT... DRIFT AWAY.
BY THE TIME I WAS IN HIGH SCHOOL HE'D QUIT HIS JOB AT THE BANK AND STARTED WORKING AT HOME.
IT WAS WEIRD HAVING HIM HOME ALL DAY... DOWN THERE IN HIS LITTLE SMOKE-FILLED OFFICE.
YOU MIND CHANGING THE CHANNEL? I'M FED UP WITH THIS SHIT.
HOW ABOUT CHANNEL TWO? LOOKS LIKE AN OLD MOVIE OR SOMETHING.
NAW... KEEP GOING.

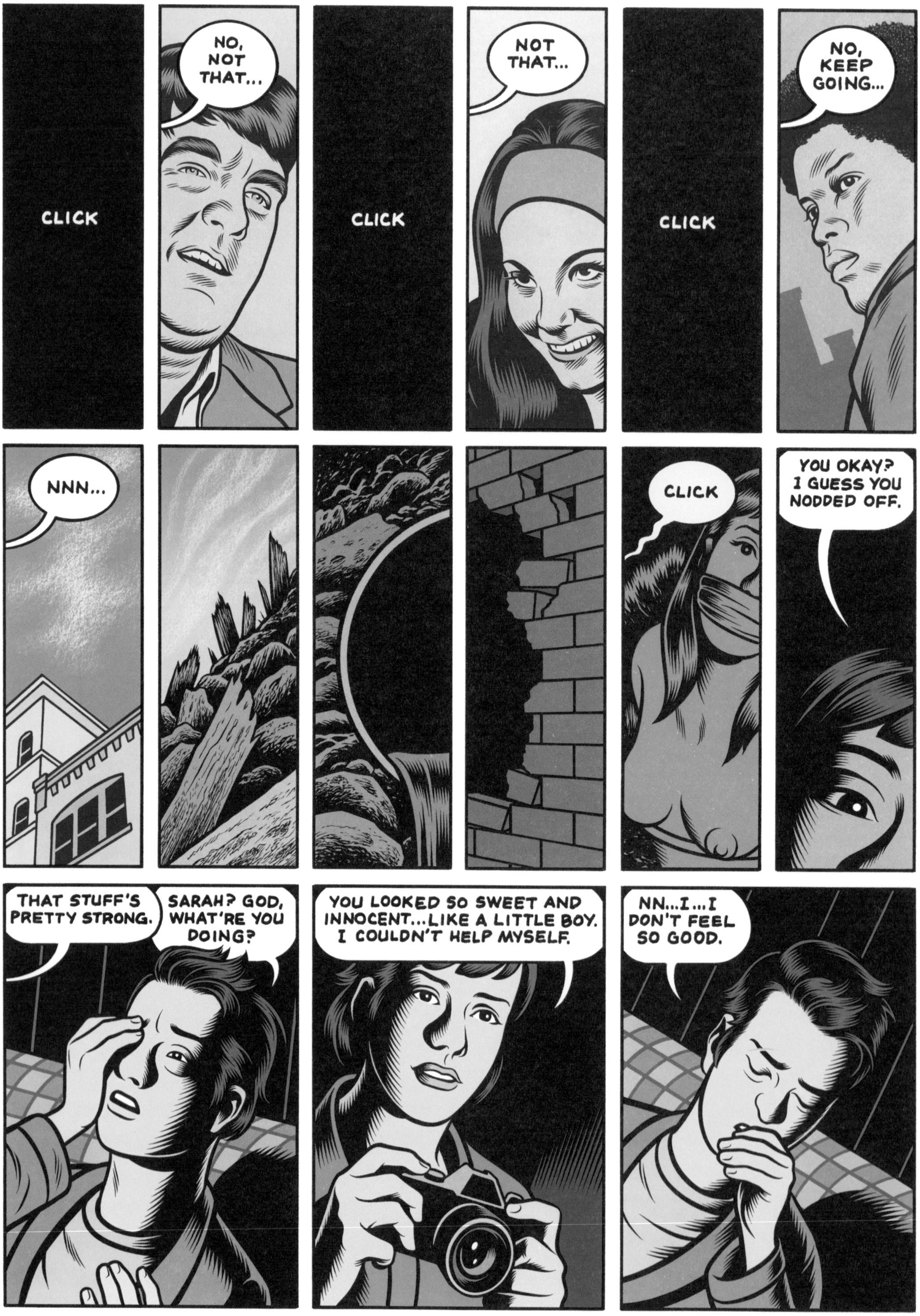
CLICK
NO, NOT THAT...
CLICK
NOT THAT...
CLICK
NO, KEEP GOING...
NNN...
CLICK
YOU OKAY? I GUESS YOU NODDED OFF.
THAT STUFF'S PRETTY STRONG.
SARAH? GOD, WHAT'RE YOU DOING?
YOU LOOKED SO SWEET AND INNOCENT...LIKE A LITTLE BOY. I COULDN'T HELP MYSELF.
NN...I...I DON'T FEEL SO GOOD.

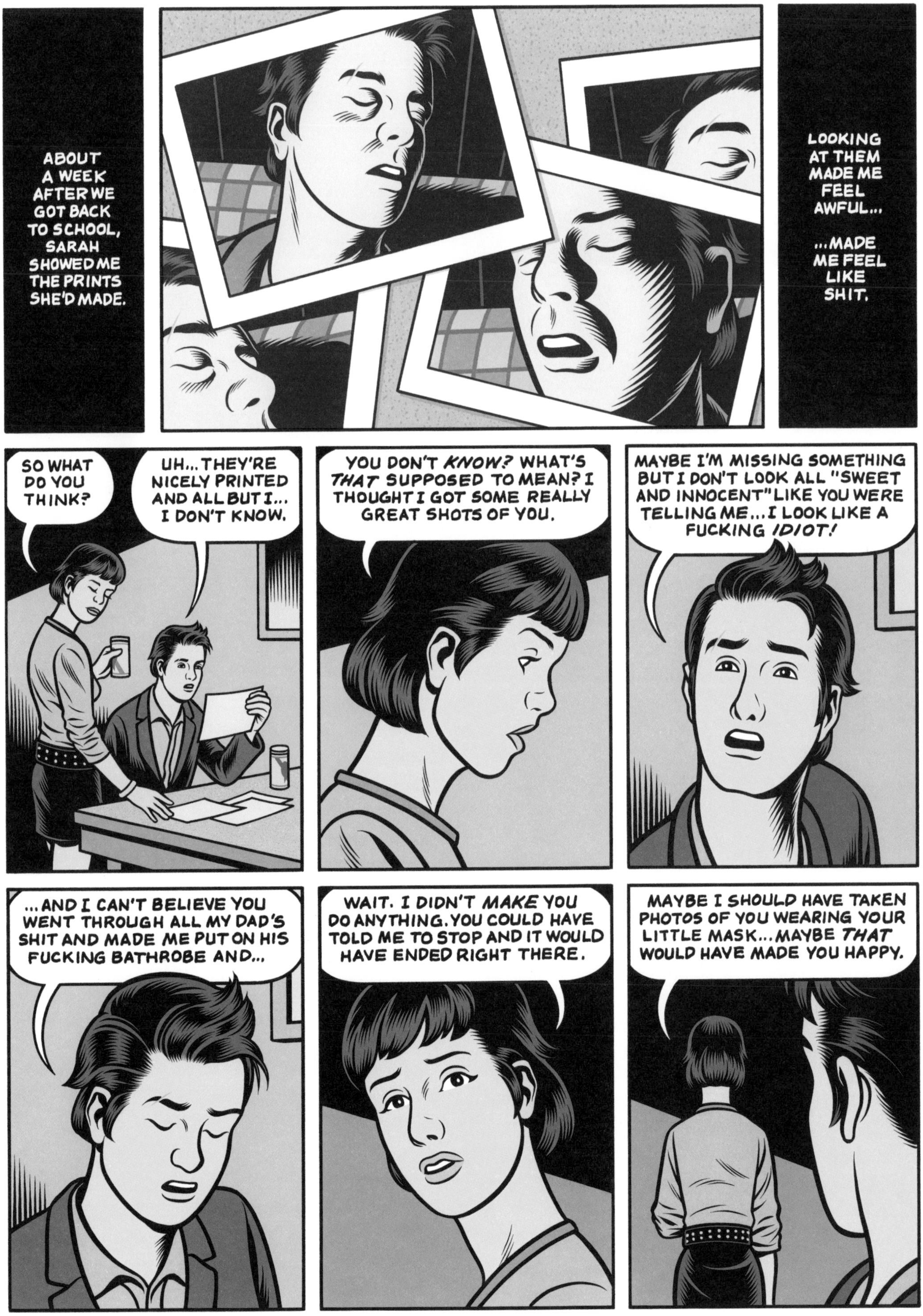
ABOUT A WEEK AFTER WE GOT BACK TO SCHOOL, SARAH SHOWED ME THE PRINTS SHE'D MADE.
LOOKING AT THEM MADE ME FEEL AWFUL...
...MADE ME FEEL LIKE SHIT.
SO WHAT DO YOU THINK?
UH... THEY'RE NICELY PRINTED AND ALL BUT I... I DON'T KNOW.
YOU DON'T KNOW? WHAT'S THAT SUPPOSED TO MEAN? I THOUGHT I GOT SOME REALLY GREAT SHOTS OF YOU.
MAYBE I'M MISSING SOMETHING BUT I DON'T LOOK ALL "SWEET AND INNOCENT" LIKE YOU WERE TELLING ME... I LOOK LIKE A FUCKING IDIOT!
...AND I CAN'T BELIEVE YOU WENT THROUGH ALL MY DAD'S SHIT AND MADE ME PUT ON HIS FUCKING BATHROBE AND...
WAIT. I DIDN'T MAKE YOU DO ANYTHING. YOU COULD HAVE TOLD ME TO STOP AND IT WOULD HAVE ENDED RIGHT THERE.
MAYBE I SHOULD HAVE TAKEN PHOTOS OF YOU WEARING YOUR LITTLE MASK... MAYBE THAT WOULD HAVE MADE YOU HAPPY.

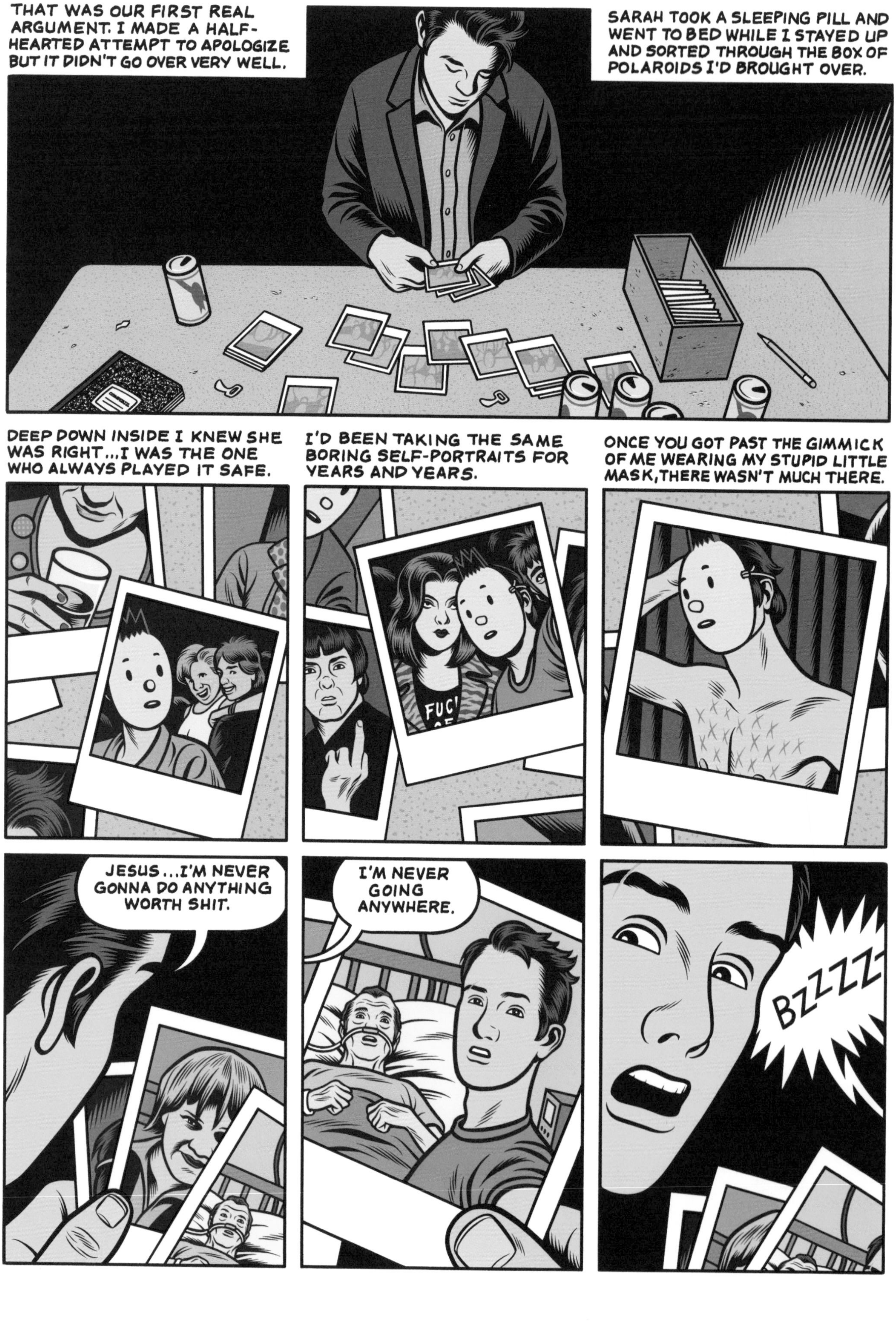
THAT WAS OUR FIRST REAL ARGUMENT. I MADE A HALF-HEARTED ATTEMPT TO APOLOGIZE BUT IT DIDN'T GO OVER VERY WELL.
SARAH TOOK A SLEEPING PILL AND WENT TO BED WHILE I STAYED UP AND SORTED THROUGH THE BOX OF POLAROIDS I'D BROUGHT OVER.
DEEP DOWN INSIDE I KNEW SHE WAS RIGHT... I WAS THE ONE WHO ALWAYS PLAYED IT SAFE.
I'D BEEN TAKING THE SAME BORING SELF-PORTRAITS FOR YEARS AND YEARS.
ONCE YOU GOT PAST THE GIMMICK OF ME WEARING MY STUPID LITTLE MASK, THERE WASN'T MUCH THERE.
JESUS... I'M NEVER GONNA DO ANYTHING WORTH SHIT.
I'M NEVER GOING ANYWHERE.
BZZZZ-

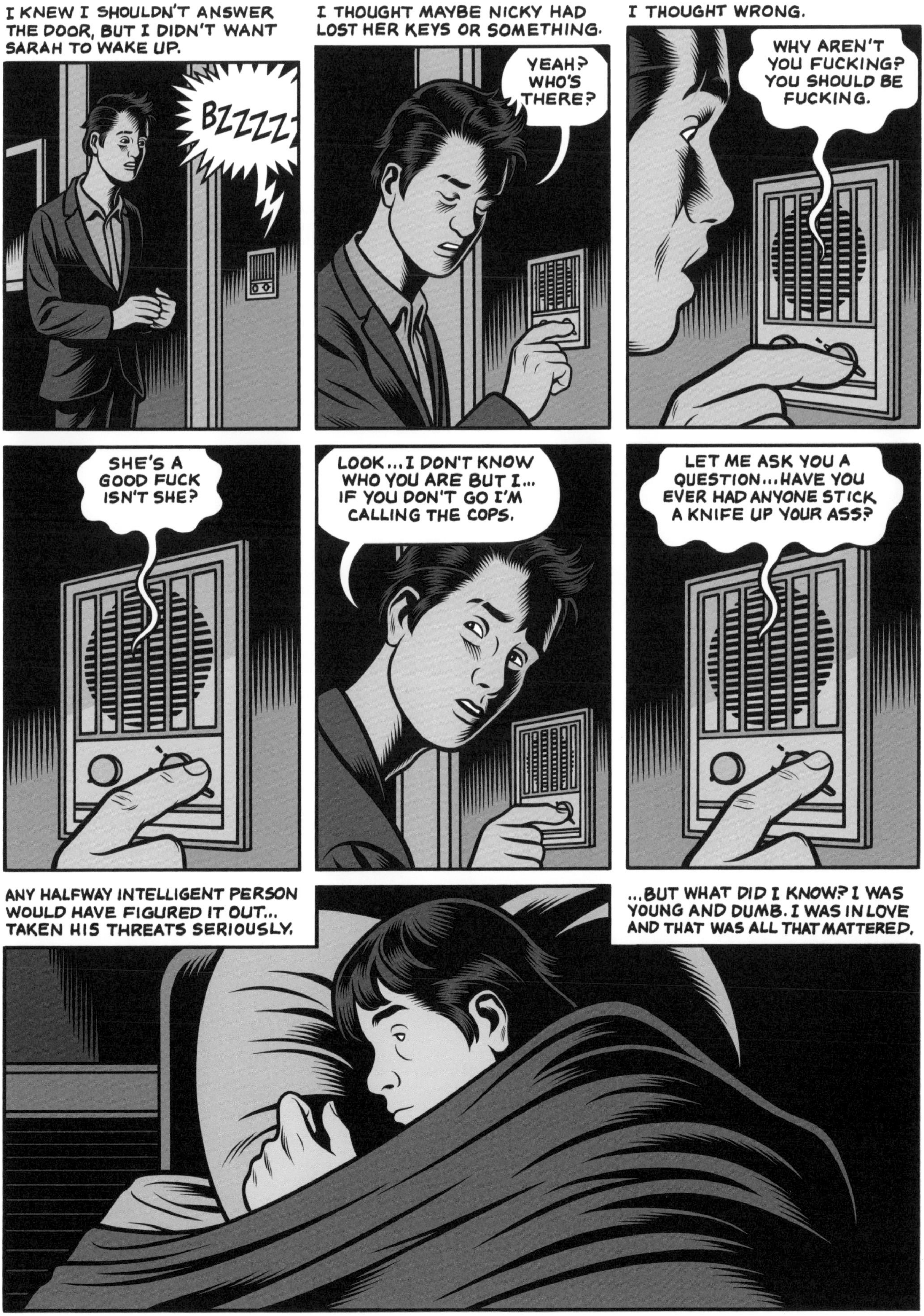
I KNEW I SHOULDN'T ANSWER THE DOOR, BUT I DIDN'T WANT SARAH TO WAKE UP.
BZZZZ
I THOUGHT MAYBE NICKY HAD LOST HER KEYS OR SOMETHING.
YEAH? WHO'S THERE?
I THOUGHT WRONG.
WHY AREN'T YOU FUCKING? YOU SHOULD BE FUCKING.
SHE'S A GOOD FUCK ISN'T SHE?
LOOK... I DON'T KNOW WHO YOU ARE BUT I... IF YOU DON'T GO I'M CALLING THE COPS.
LET ME ASK YOU A QUESTION... HAVE YOU EVER HAD ANYONE STICK A KNIFE UP YOUR ASS?
ANY HALFWAY INTELLIGENT PERSON WOULD HAVE FIGURED IT OUT... TAKEN HIS THREATS SERIOUSLY.
...BUT WHAT DID I KNOW? I WAS YOUNG AND DUMB. I WAS IN LOVE AND THAT WAS ALL THAT MATTERED.

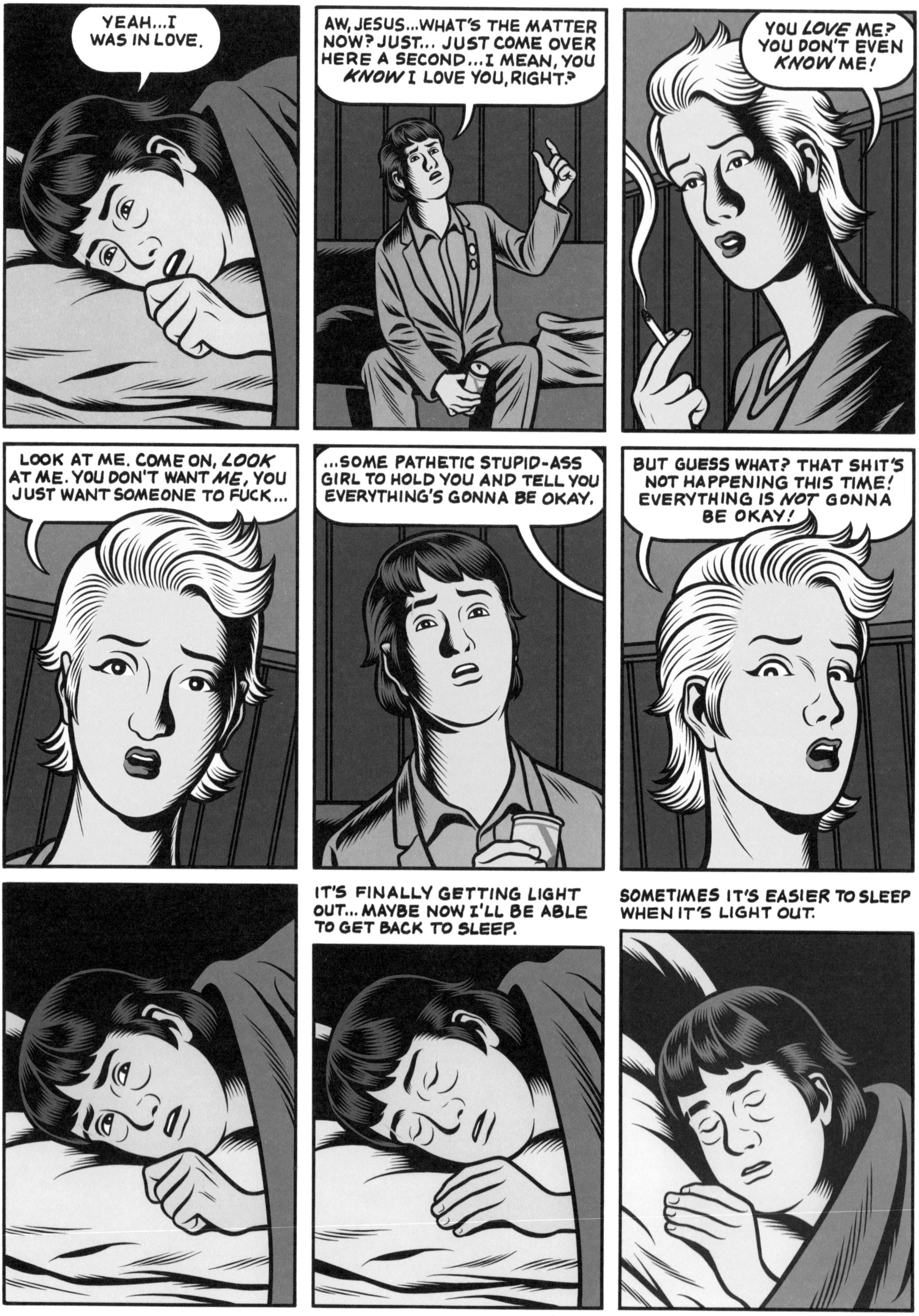
YEAH...I WAS IN LOVE.
AW, JESUS...WHAT'S THE MATTER NOW? JUST... JUST COME OVER HERE A SECOND...I MEAN, YOU *KNOW* I LOVE YOU, RIGHT?
YOU *LOVE* ME? YOU DON'T EVEN *KNOW* ME!
LOOK AT ME. COME ON, *LOOK* AT ME. YOU DON'T WANT *ME*, YOU JUST WANT SOMEONE TO FUCK...
...SOME PATHETIC STUPID-ASS GIRL TO HOLD YOU AND TELL YOU EVERYTHING'S GONNA BE OKAY.
BUT GUESS WHAT? THAT SHIT'S NOT HAPPENING THIS TIME! EVERYTHING IS *NOT* GONNA BE OKAY!
IT'S FINALLY GETTING LIGHT OUT... MAYBE NOW I'LL BE ABLE TO GET BACK TO SLEEP.
SOMETIMES IT'S EASIER TO SLEEP WHEN IT'S LIGHT OUT.

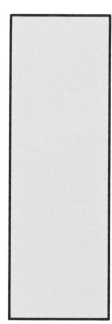

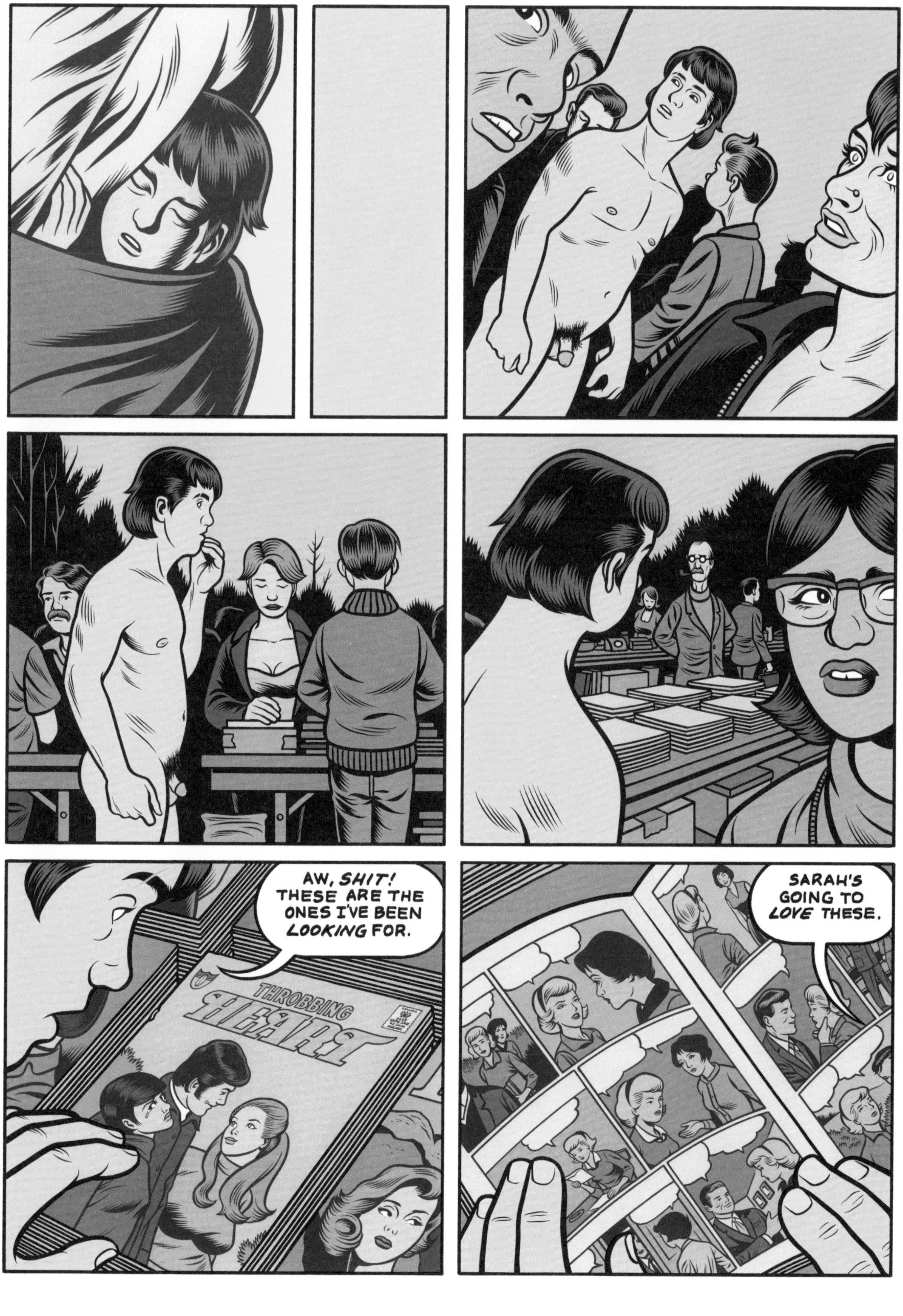
AW, SHIT! THESE ARE THE ONES I'VE BEEN LOOKING FOR.
THROBBING HEART
SARAH'S GOING TO LOVE THESE.

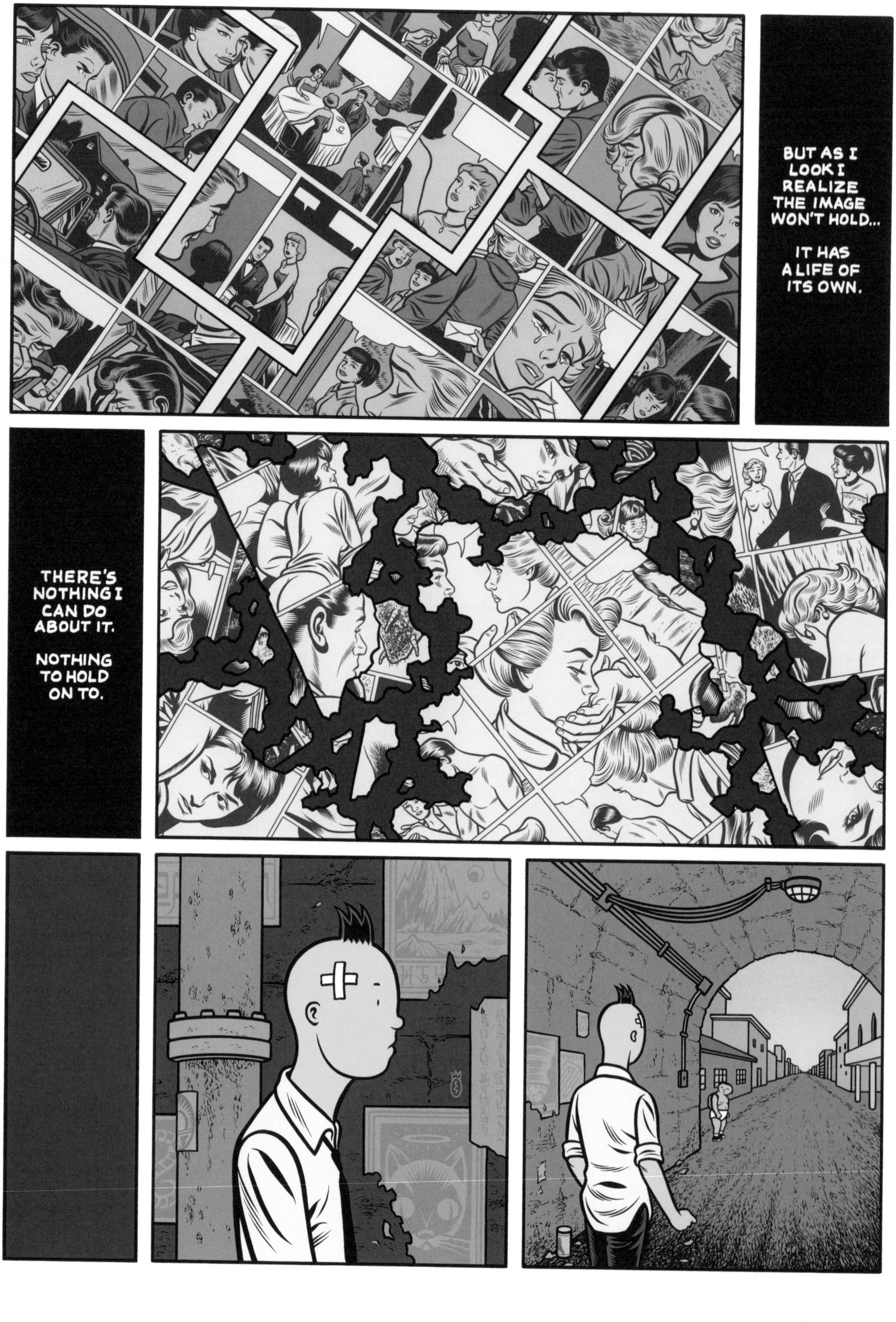
BUT AS I LOOK I REALIZE THE IMAGE WON'T HOLD...
IT HAS A LIFE OF ITS OWN.
THERE'S NOTHING I CAN DO ABOUT IT.
NOTHING TO HOLD ON TO.

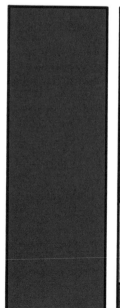

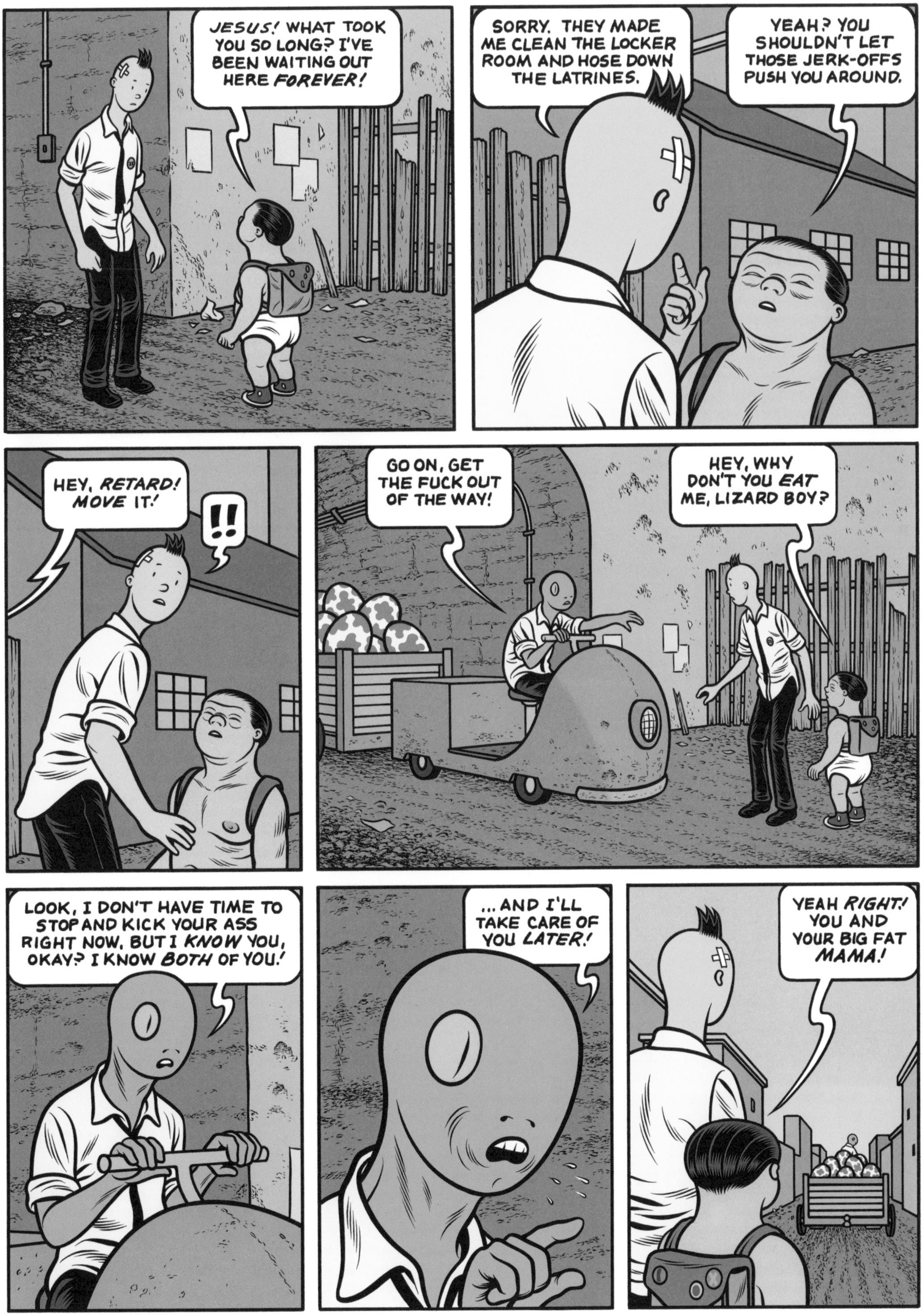
JESUS! WHAT TOOK YOU SO LONG? I'VE BEEN WAITING OUT HERE FOREVER!
SORRY. THEY MADE ME CLEAN THE LOCKER ROOM AND HOSE DOWN THE LATRINES.
YEAH? YOU SHOULDN'T LET THOSE JERK-OFFS PUSH YOU AROUND.
HEY, RETARD! MOVE IT!
!!
GO ON, GET THE FUCK OUT OF THE WAY!
HEY, WHY DON'T YOU EAT ME, LIZARD BOY?
LOOK, I DON'T HAVE TIME TO STOP AND KICK YOUR ASS RIGHT NOW, BUT I KNOW YOU, OKAY? I KNOW BOTH OF YOU!
...AND I'LL TAKE CARE OF YOU LATER!
YEAH RIGHT! YOU AND YOUR BIG FAT MAMA!

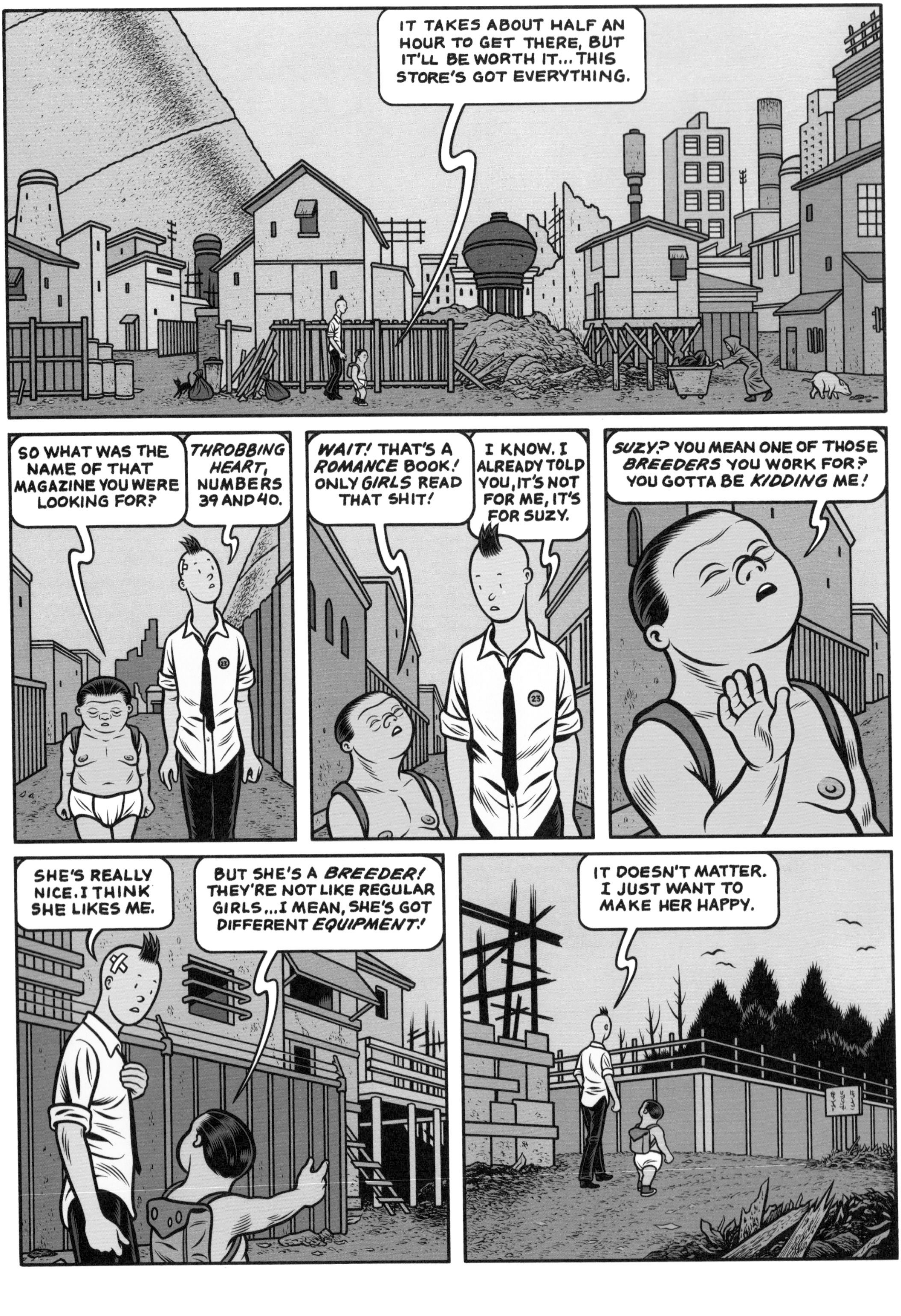
IT TAKES ABOUT HALF AN HOUR TO GET THERE, BUT IT'LL BE WORTH IT... THIS STORE'S GOT EVERYTHING.
SO WHAT WAS THE NAME OF THAT MAGAZINE YOU WERE LOOKING FOR?
THROBBING HEART, NUMBERS 39 AND 40.
WAIT! THAT'S A ROMANCE BOOK! ONLY GIRLS READ THAT SHIT!
I KNOW. I ALREADY TOLD YOU, IT'S NOT FOR ME, IT'S FOR SUZY.
SUZY? YOU MEAN ONE OF THOSE BREEDERS YOU WORK FOR? YOU GOTTA BE KIDDING ME!
SHE'S REALLY NICE. I THINK SHE LIKES ME.
BUT SHE'S A BREEDER! THEY'RE NOT LIKE REGULAR GIRLS... I MEAN, SHE'S GOT DIFFERENT EQUIPMENT!
IT DOESN'T MATTER. I JUST WANT TO MAKE HER HAPPY.

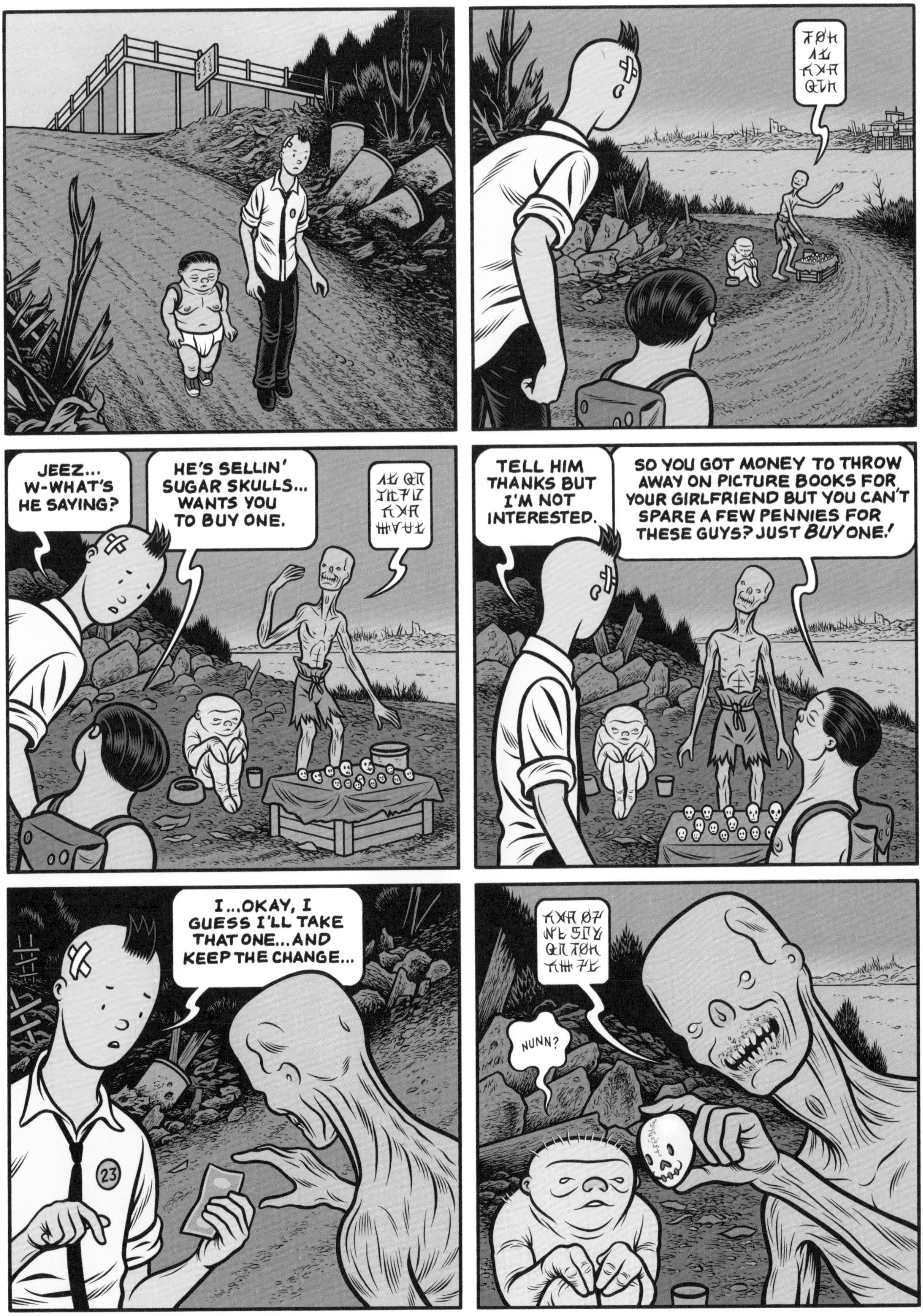
JEEZ... W-WHAT'S HE SAYING?
HE'S SELLIN' SUGAR SKULLS... WANTS YOU TO BUY ONE.
TELL HIM THANKS BUT I'M NOT INTERESTED.
SO YOU GOT MONEY TO THROW AWAY ON PICTURE BOOKS FOR YOUR GIRLFRIEND BUT YOU CAN'T SPARE A FEW PENNIES FOR THESE GUYS? JUST *BUY* ONE!
I...OKAY, I GUESS I'LL TAKE THAT ONE...AND KEEP THE CHANGE...
23
NUNN?

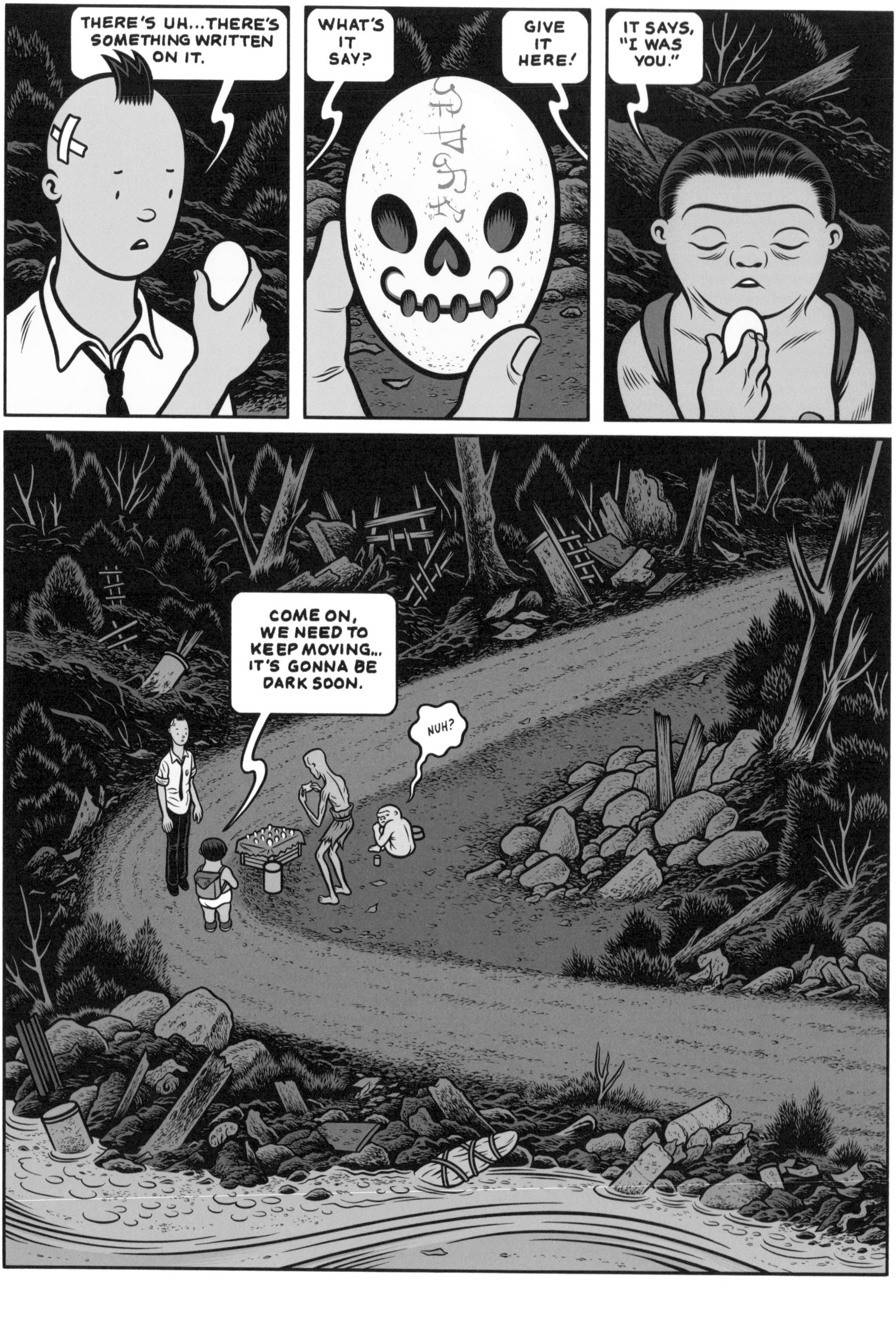
THERE'S UH... THERE'S SOMETHING WRITTEN ON IT.
WHAT'S IT SAY?
GIVE IT HERE!
IT SAYS, "I WAS YOU."
COME ON, WE NEED TO KEEP MOVING... IT'S GONNA BE DARK SOON.
NUH?

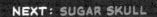

NEXT: SUGAR SKULL

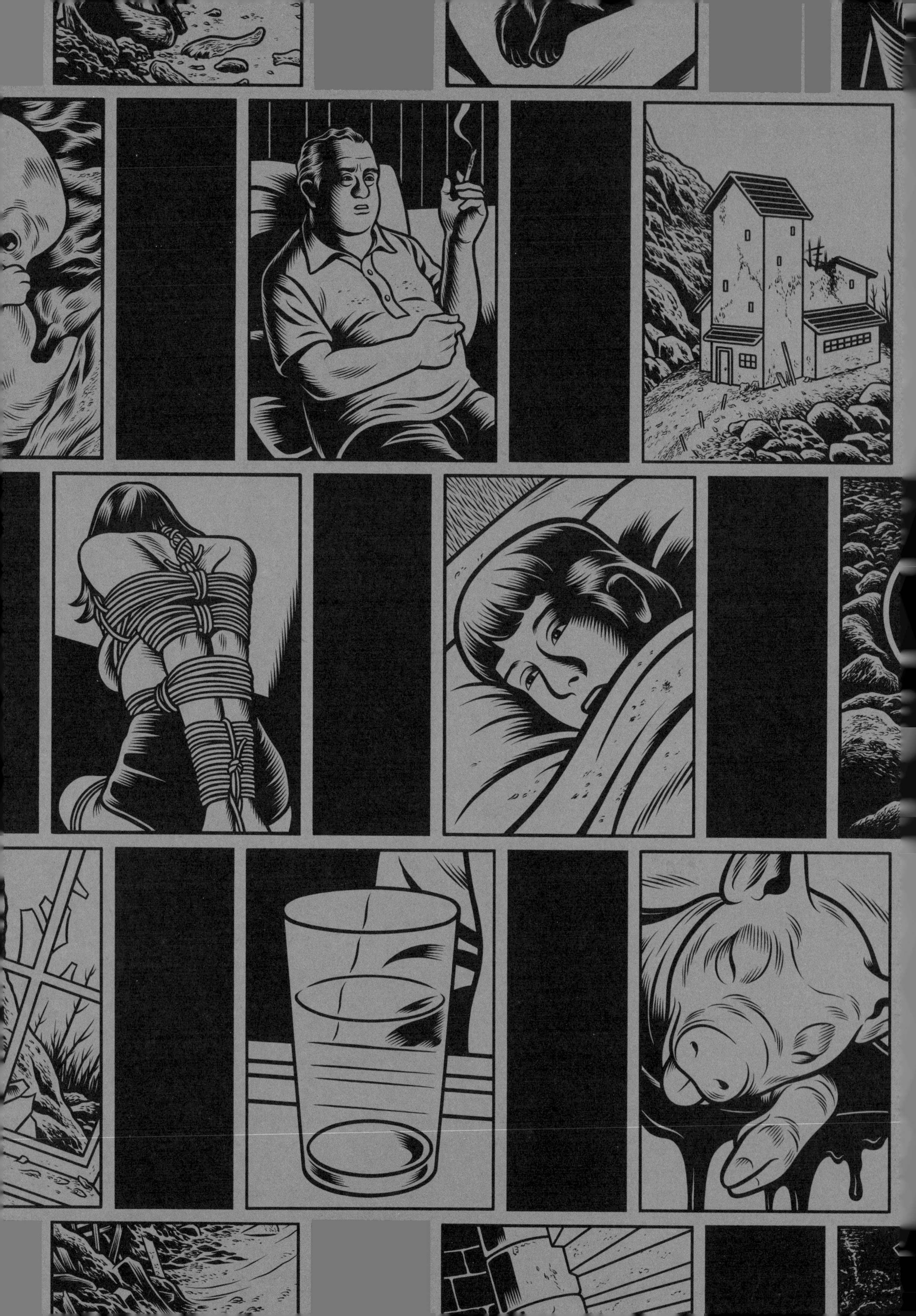